PERIL BENEATH THE SURFACE

JOHN LYNCH

JOHN LYNCH
HIGH EXPLOSIVE HORROR

PRAISE FOR JOHN LYNCH

John Lynch isn't here to mess around… and neither is his fiction. Every word, every sentence, is a well-placed bullseye from a sharpshooter of a writer.

— BRIAN KEENE, AUTHOR OF *THE RISING*

For everyone reading this book. Thank you.

PROLOGUE

They sat along the shore of the lake, where last week, according to triangulation done by seismologists, the strongest earthquake Rhode Island had ever experienced took place—smack-dab in the center of the lake. Nothing looked different. No damage reported, no environmental issues because of the earthquake. Despite the excitement of the population over the historical event, people soon forgot. In the age of TikTok and Reels people were soon on to the next news item.

Sabrina took a long hit of the blunt, pulling smoke into her lungs. She held it there until her chest ached and just before she could no longer resist the urge to cough, she exhaled. "That's some good shit," she said, holding the long brown object between her thumb and index finger.

Paula giggled. "If it's so good, why are you trying to pass it to me? You know the rules. Pufff, puff, pass when it's just the two of us."

Sabrina eyed the dutch with contempt. "Because you

know I hate these things, they taste horrible. Why can't you smoke a bowl like normal people?"

"But it's vanilla, I thought they were your favorite? And you know I like to roll them, itt relaxes me."

"What I *said* was I can tolerate it. Do you have a favorite flavor of dog shit?"

Paula burst out laughing.

Sabrina had a way of saying things in a monotone, dry inflection that left most people questioning if she was serious, no matter how outlandish the comment. But not Paula. Paula understood her, and that was part of what Sabrina loved about her. She never had to explain herself, it was already understood. And the way she laughed with her entire body was cute, and sent butterflies throughout Sabrina's stomach.

She joined Paula laughing hysterically.

"Here, take this thing before I drop it," she managed to say between heaves of laughter. Her cheeks were warm and she felt something wet drip down them. It felt amazing to laugh, laugh herself to tears. She seemed to do less and less of that these days.

But it was a feeling Sabrina knew would not stick around. After they graduated, they'd agreed to take a semester off to decide what they were going to do, and frankly, to enjoy themselves. That had been Paula's idea, of course. Sabrina had wanted to jump right into school, keep the momentum going. She didn't see how it made sense to put it off for later. High school was a pain in the ass as it was, college, she expected, would be much more serious, so it seemed to her like the smarter play would be to jump right in while you were used to the grind of formal education.

But Paula had convinced her otherwise. She was good at making you see the flip side of the coin, and though Sabrina hadn't agreed immediately, Paula was quite persistent, pecking away at Sabrina's resolve until she became open to the idea of taking time off. The clincher was the way Paula described life going forward, convincing her that the moment they enrolled in college they would become cogs in the machine. Their lives would become a boring string of long days filled with school and work, waiting for the weekend, and then being too exhausted from the week to enjoy it. Only to repeat the process again and again, until they eventually retired, most likely at an age when they'd be too old to actually enjoy life.

And then they would die, bitter and miserable that they hadn't truly enjoyed life. Maybe if they were one of the lucky ones they might land a sweet job that delivered a better work/life balance and they'd be happy. But those were the outliers in life. You only had to look around at how miserable 99 percent of adults were to realize that. The way things were going these days, especially in Rhode Island, the odds of being one of the happy ones seemed to grow slimmer by the day.

Paula didn't want that for herself, and she'd done a bang up job of convincing Sabrina.

One semester off turned into two, and now the end of the spring semester was fast approaching and Sabrina knew things had changed. Even if she hadn't gone through Paula's phone, even if she hadn't seen the letters from different schools, Paula hadn't been her usual self. She'd grown distant, which was completely unlike her. They'd been together their entire time at high school, only ever dating each other.

Sabrina knew enough about Paula to know that their time together was coming to an end.

Ruminating on the impending breakup—even if it had yet to be acknowledged by either of them—deflated her good spirits.

Paula snatched the dutch. "More for me then, bitch," she said, giggling again.

Sabrina hated it when Paula couldn't read her mood. It was a constant point of contention for them. Paula would always say she's not a mind reader, so how was she supposed to know something was wrong? But she should know, dammit. They'd been together forever, how could she *not* know?

Her mood soured as Paula laughed, completely unaware that Sabrina was upset. But this was almost the end for them; Sabrina recognized this and decided to let it go. Why spoil what time they had left together? She would want to look back fondly on these days. Days when they were no longer children but hadn't quite taken the leap to adulthood. Days before life would slowly beat them down, drain their livelihoods, and rob them of their innocence.

"It's all yours. I'm too high right now to take another hit," Sabrina said. She stood up and stretched, reaching for the stars.

It was a beautiful night, the moon was high, the sky clear. Out on the lake, the man-made luminescence of civilization did little to disrupt stargazing.

Paula stood up, joining her girlfriend. "It's beautiful, isn't it?"

"Yeah."

"What are you thinking about?" Paula asked.

Sabrina's ears burned red hot; she didn't want to talk

about it. The one time Paula had sensed something wrong. Talk about luck. "Nothing," Sabrina said.

"Well, instead of thinking about nothing, you could think about this ass," Paula said, dropping her denim shorts onto the sand, revealing a bright pink bikini bottom that left little to the imagination.

"You're crazy," Sabrina said, "it's freezing."

"Sab, shut up and come with me." Paula ran to the water, peeling her top off and tossing it aside.

Sabrina watched, admiring Paula's physique. They'd explored each other's bodies many times, as young lovers do. Seeing her like this, Sabrina wondered how many more times they'd get the chance. Any night could be their last before they went their separate ways. Would tonight be their last? "Fuck it," she said, stripping down to her swimsuit and following Paula. By the time Sabrina made it to the waterline, Paula had already gone so far from shore the water licked at her collarbone.

The lake was cold this time of the year, and would remain so for a few more months before warming up. Sabrina stepped in and flinched, letting out a hiss. The water was every bit as cold as she anticipated.

"I heard that!" Paula shouted. "Just run in, the quicker you get wet, the quicker you'll get used to it. Besides, that will give me an excuse to warm you up in the car."

Fuck it, Sabrina thought. *Even if this isn't our last night, it will be one of our last memories together.* She ran in, joining her girlfriend.

A few inches shorter than Paula, by the time Sabrina made it out to where her girlfriend awaited her, the water was up to her chin. She looked up at Paula—her face only just above the water—and smiled. Paula leaned down, embraced her. They kissed. Just the lips at first, then a flick of the tongue. Sabrina pressed her toes into the bottom of the lake, trying to lean harder into the kiss but it was difficult when the water was almost covering her entire face.

Paula pushed off her and floated backward, laughing. "You gotta come get me if you want me," she said.

"C'mon, Paula, the water is already up to my chin," Sabrina said.

"You can swim, can't you? Besides, you can trust me, I wouldn't let anything bad happen, baby."

The moment the words escaped her lips, Paula slipped below the surface without another word. It sounded as if maybe she'd made a little squeak, a noise of surprise, but with all the water in Sabrina's ears, she couldn't be sure what she heard. She slipped through the water so quietly that if Sabrina hadn't been watching, she would have had no clue Paula had gone under.

"Stop fucking around, you know I don't want to swim out that far," Sabrina said, knowing Paula couldn't hear her beneath the still, cold water of the lake. She dipped below the surface for a moment, opened her eyes. Nothing but blackness. Not a chance in hell Sabrina could see what Paula was doing; she could barely see her hands in front of her.

Why did Paula have to do this? Why couldn't they have a *normal* night? Sabrina didn't want to play this game. It was too cold and she was grumpy, only just managing to put her anxiety toward the future aside in order to enjoy a night she knew was one of only a finite number of nights like tonight. *Why bother? I should just go back to shore and make her come to me.*

It didn't occur to Sabrina how long Paula had been

underwater until a loud splash broke her train of thought and she saw Paula's arm claw up from the depths. A soul-piercing shriek erupted from her, a primal sound Sabrina wouldn't have pegged as coming from a human without having witnessed it firsthand.

"Help!" Paula screamed. "Please, help me!"

Sabrina's heart pounded in her chest; she could feel blood thrumming in her ears as panic set in. She swam toward her girlfriend, not knowing what to expect. Was she drowning? Had she swallowed water or something? She noticed Paula treading water but she was freaking out. A good swimmer, yes, but how long could she keep that up?

Closer now, it looked like she was peeling at her face, half of which was darker than the other half. Was she bleeding? There weren't jellyfish in these waters, right?

Paula dipped under again and came back up. Sabrina was closer now and her initial thought had been spot on—there was something covering Paula's face.

Not blood, something darker. Thicker.

Paula's screams grew more frantic, somehow more terrible than before. She clawed at her face again, and part of the dark substance peeled away, stuck to her hand.

Paula's eye was missing, plucked from the socket. All Sabrina could see was a dark pit with a bit of dangling, frayed optic nerve hanging from it.

"Oh my fucking God," Sabrina said as she turned and swam away, her instinct for survival taking precedence over her concern for her girlfriend. Whatever the fuck that shit on Paula was, she wasn't about to get on herself. She swam faster, even as the dark ooze-thing continued ravaging her girlfriend.

On Paula's hand, a tendril grew from the separated

section of the substance. Then lightning quick, it sling-shotted itself at Paula's face, rejoining the larger portion of the substance.

The black substance undulated, its surface rippling as it changed shapes and forms, at times seeming to take on the appearance of the various lake-dwelling creatures it had consumed. The thing reverted back to its fluidlike form and in the blink of an eye, spread along Paula's body.

Sabrina, at the water's edge now, crawled ashore. She coughed so hard she felt she was hacking up a lung. Lake water spewed from her mouth. Though she hadn't been in danger of drowning, during her panicked swim ashore she swallowed a good amount of water. Her entire body ached. Chest, lungs, limbs, all burning from exhaustion. She scrambled to her feet, turned around.

The lake was still, the woods eerily quiet.

Paula was gone.

Sabrina broke down. Safe from whatever the fuck was in the lake, her brain and body refused to comply with her gut feeling that she needed to get the hell out of there and call the police.

Minutes that felt like hours passed before her sobs subsided enough to stop racking her body. She never saw the black substance creep out of the lake, slithering through the sand until it began to reshape itself a few feet in front of her. When she finally saw the ooze, she screamed. Scrambling to her feet, she took off running toward the car.

The black ooze was now in the rough shape of a human being. Its features were not clearly defined but the shape was unmistakable. Head, shoulders, feet—all human. It writhed and tumbled and ran along itself, like a mass of black maggots forming one large organism.

Sabrina reached the driver's-side door as the thing stalked toward her, globs of goop plopping to the ground as it moved quicker now, seemingly adjusted to bipedal locomotion. She pulled the handle, opened the door, slid behind the wheel, and locked herself in.

She pushed the *START ENGINE* button but had forgotten to grab the keys out of Paula's shorts. "Shit, shit, shit," she said, slamming her fist onto the steering wheel, punctuating each profanity. How could she be so stupid?

Outside the car, the creature pounded the glass with an arm that, at some point while Sabrina was trying to start the vehicle, had transformed from a human limb into something closer to a club-like blunt object. The car shook violently, the window spiderwebbed.

Sabrina looked at the monstrosity and screamed. Even if she hadn't seen what it had done to Paula, she'd still be terrified. It looked like a child's crude drawing of a featureless woman. Except that wasn't quite right, there were features, but they weren't well-defined. Sabrina thought she could almost see Paula. Had the thing imitated her? What the fuck could do something like that?

She screamed again and the humanoid thing lost its shape, dropping out of sight.

Her heart hammering in her chest, pulse racing, Sabrina gasped for air. She didn't know what to do. Was it gone? Why had it just disappeared like that? She wasn't sure if she should run to grab the keys out of Paula's shorts or stay here until someone came looking for the couple. Surely someone would, right? Sabrina hadn't told anyone where they were going, though. Had Paula? The lake was deserted most of the year, with much of the land now owned by one person. The few homes that were owned by other private parties wouldn't be inhabited at this time of the year. They were vacation homes, vacant until the summer months.

If Paula hadn't told anyone where they were, it might be some time before someone discovered them.

She had no choice but to make a run for the keys and hope whatever the hell that thing was, was gone.

Sabrina took a deep breath, trying, unsuccessfully, to calm her nerves. She steeled herself, grabbed the handle, and shoved the door open.

But it didn't budge. "What the fuck!" she said, rattling the door as she continued pulling the handle. It was no use; the door was jammed.

Outside the car, the ooze had spread from the undercarriage to the body of the vehicle, slowly enveloping the entire thing. It crept slowly, working its way up until it had reached the windows.

When at last Sabrina saw the black ooze spreading along all the windows, her mind snapped and the windows imploded. Jagged shards of glass raining down upon her from all angles.

The substance worked its way up Sabrina's body, eating away at the organic tissue.

It wasn't until the ooze penetrated her mouth, suffocating her, that Sabrina stopped screaming.

1

Tommy shot up, arms and legs flailing. His body's movement was restricted by the cocoon-like sleeping bag. The sudden urge to piss himself so prominent it woke him from his sleep. His seventeen-year-old bladder was no match for the excessive consumption of energy drinks he'd pounded with his best friend, Joey.

Tommy unzipped the bag and clawed his way out. From the corner of his eye, he noticed Joey's bag was empty. "Fuck," he said, "he better not be in the bathroom."

With sleep-blurred vision, Tommy lurched toward the bedroom door and tripped over a pile of dirty laundry. He stumbled out of his room into the hallway, regaining his balance at the last moment and narrowly avoiding face-planting against the wall directly across from his bedroom.

The Ross family had lived in the same home for most of Tommy's life, and he knew the layout like the back of his hand. Still, he crept like a thief in the night, using his fingers for guidance. He didn't need help finding the bathroom, but another stumble like the one in his bedroom would cause too much noise and wake his father. That wouldn't be good. With all the noise they'd made late into the night, his father had been so pissed-off Tommy was surprised the man hadn't come upstairs and beat the brakes off him already. There would be an awful lot of ass kissing in his future to get back in good graces.

Tommy didn't consider what his father did abuse, even if others might. It wasn't as if he beat his son regularly. He never had to take days off from school for "accidents," like some of the kids he went to school with. But sometimes, when Tommy acted a fool, his father would put his hands to work, teaching his son a lesson. The first time, his father had said, "Whenever you get the idea to do something stupid, you'll think about this, and then you'll think a bit harder and ask yourself if whatever dumb shit you're up to is worth the risk."

And his father had been right. For the most part, Tommy was a good kid and avoided the trouble many of his peers found themselves in. It wasn't that he was a Goody Two-shoes, or anything like that. Tommy still smoked weed, still drank, still got into his fair share of questionable activities. The difference was that Tommy made sure the times when he *was* going to get up to no good, it was highly unlikely it would come back to bite him in the ass.

Or maybe he was overthinking things. Sure, he'd pissed his old man off, but maybe his father understood that the school year was all but over and both his son, and his son's best friend tested exceptionally well on their SATs and deserved a bit of a celebration. And all things considered, hanging out watching movies and playing video games was a pretty fucking tame celebration. If anything, his father should be happy he wasn't out causing trouble and doing anything that would put his future in jeopardy. Lord knew there were plenty of parties every weekend, opportunities to get up to no good.

Even half asleep, creeping to take a leak, Tommy's mind wandered toward the future. The only thing standing between him and a college life full of beautiful women, crazy parties, and plenty of mind-altering substances— without the worry of an ass whooping hanging over his shoulder—was the upcoming summer break. A summer break he hoped would carry more excitement than tonight's celebration. As much as he enjoyed nights like this, staying up late, binge-watching horror movies, and playing video games, he longed for the exhilarating nights many of his classmates experienced, but he always had the specter of his father's approval looming over his shoulder. Even his sister, Jackie, had the balls to risk their father's wrath. Although to be fair, his twin sister was Dad's favorite. He was wrapped around her finger and everyone knew it. There would be no repercussions for any of her misdeeds, a fact that chapped Tommy's ass. Jackie was a Daddy's girl, through and through.

After skulking around in the dark for what seemed like an eternity, Tommy reached the bathroom door. Immediately he noticed it was empty. The door wide open, all lights off. So where was Joey? That was a question for later, because if Tommy didn't piss within the next few moments his junk might explode.

He stood over the toilet, leaning forward with one hand propped against the wall. The other hand guiding the strong flow of pungent piss into the bowl. There was something satisfying about a good, long leak. In Tommy's short time on Earth, the only thing that compared was the final moments of masturbation, the moment of relief that so many teenage boys looked upon as a religious experience, so much so that their days were spent jacking off, finding new ways to jack off, and thinking about the next time they might be able to jack off.

The deed finished, Tommy shook himself off. Two shakes, to be exact. Enough to be rid of any stray droplet, but not enough to be accused of flogging his log. As he tucked himself back into his shorts, he noticed the highlighter yellow color in the toilet. His piss practically glowed.

I'd better drink some water with breakfast.

Tommy flushed the toilet, washed his hands, and exited the bathroom.

He took a few steps and noticed his sister's door cracked open. Not much, but it struck him as odd. Before leaving for the evening, Jackie had made it a point to let Tommy know her door was shut and was to remain shut until she came home. And should she find out her door was open at any time while she was gone, Tommy's secret porn stash wouldn't be so secret anymore. Mom would see her baby boy in a whole new light. He knew he should throw them out, especially in the age of smartphones where there was really no need to have magazines. There was an entire world of naked women at his fingertips, but something about flipping through the pages appealed to him in a way that scrolling a porn site for thirty minutes to find the right video simply did not.

Tommy didn't doubt that his sister would make good on the threat, and honestly, he didn't really care if his mother found out. Unless she lived under a rock, she had to know that her teenage son, with unrestricted internet access on his phone, was beating his dick like it owed him money. Of course he had a stash of porn hidden away in the files of his phone, for those times when he wouldn't have the privacy to sit back with his feet up reading a magazine. Half the memory on the phone was dedicated to women in various states of undress.

The real reason he didn't go into his sister's room was simple. There was nothing there for him. Nothing tempting him. He didn't care what secrets she hid in there—there had to be some, all teens hide secrets. He harbored no interest in hidden journals, stashed money, or the marijuana hidden inside a shoebox she kept tucked away in the back of her closet.

Joey, on the other hand . . . Who knew what ideas were running through his head? The fog fully cleared from his mind, it occurred to Tommy why the door was cracked. It hadn't opened on its own, and Jackie hadn't mistakenly left it open. Nope. His best friend was being a disgusting little perv, and he didn't need to catch him in the act to come to *that* conclusion. Although he wasn't going to let the opportunity to catch him slip by either.

Tommy put his eye to the crack and peered into the bedroom. No good, he couldn't see shit. It was too dark, and the crack wasn't wide enough. He strained at the door; his ears working hard to search for out-of-place noises. He heard something rustling from the far corner of the room but couldn't place the sound. Not wanting to alert Joey to his presence, Tommy quietly pushed the door open a little further, just enough to get a better view.

A blade of light from Jackie's open closet door sliced through the dark room, pooling on the carpet in front of it.

He better not be stealing her weed. She's gonna go scorched-earth if it turns up missing.

Tommy entered the room, moving quicker but still careful not to alert Joey to his presence. He made his way across the room, seeing the dollar signs floating in front of his eyes. Whatever Joey was up to, he knew he'd be able to blackmail his friend over it. A few hundred bucks going into the summer could make things much more fun. His stomach growled thinking about all the pizza he'd buy with the extra coin.

Tommy reached the closet door and flung it open, eyes wide with shock.

Joey, his best friend, was on his knees with a pair of Jackie's panties over his head, and another pair wrapped around his fist, which was pumping his cock.

"Jesus Christ, what the fuck are you doing?" Tommy asked.

"I . . . I can explain . . ."

"Before you do, why don't you stop playing with yourself and put that thing away. My sister is gonna kill you if she finds a wad of jizz in her underwear."

"I wasn't gonna do that, I swear!"

"Man, shut the fuck up. What else were you gonna do? Stop being a nasty little fucker and get the hell out of here."

Joey stood up and put his pecker back in his boxers. He shook his head and the panties fell to the floor. Slowly, he pushed the hand clutching the other pair into the pocket of his lounge pants.

Tommy saw the not-so-subtle move. "You better put her underwear back, man. That's my damn sister."

Joey's eyes bulged from his head like a cartoon character. "She's gonna know I had them."

"If you put them back where you found them, and we leave the room how it was before you decided to be a fucking deviant, she's not gonna know shit. Unless I tell her."

"You're not gonna tell her, are you?"

"Depends. How much money you got?"

"Are you fucking kidding me, dude?"

"Fine, I'll tell Jackie you were masturbating with her panties. Better yet, I'll wake my dad up and let him know."

"Okay, okay. I'll put everything back the way I found it. How much do you want, man?"

"We can negotiate later. Now get out."

Joey put Jackie's undergarments back in the dresser drawer and slid it closed. He pulled the string hanging from the ceiling, cutting the light off in an instant, bathing the room in darkness.

As the boys made their way back to the bedroom and slithered into their sleeping bags, Tommy thought of what Joey might be willing to pay. And he thought of another, much more fun idea.

If only Jackie would play ball.

2

———————

Lucy Evans walked along the tree line, just off the edge of the asphalt. It was late and the one-lane road didn't see heavy traffic, even during daylight hours, but Lucy didn't want to take any chances. Better to trudge through the tall grass with the ticks and risk Lyme disease than risk being annihilated by a driver not paying attention on a dark, deserted road in the middle of nowhere.

Walking home alone in the dark wasn't the smartest decision a young woman could make, but it was much better than the other option—spending the evening in bed with her boss, Travis.

She cursed herself for not trusting her gut instinct. Something had seemed off about the entire situation. Drinks at his place, rather than a public setting. Lucy didn't consider her relationship with Travis anything more than what it was at face value—boss and employee—so it seemed inappropriate that he would ask her to come his residence.

He must have seen the wheels turning in her head

because as soon as he'd invited her, he was quick to assure that her office coworkers and friends would be invited to the celebration as well. Reluctantly, she agreed. At least if she was among coworkers, she would be safe.

Boy, had she been wrong about that. She started to wonder if there might be some truth to all that "man vs. bear" talk.

Later that evening, after Lucy had driven home from work, she spent a bit of time getting ready. She thought about simply letting her hair down, changing her shoes to something more comfortable, and then heading over. She didn't want to give Travis, or anyone else, the wrong impression. But after debating it, Lucy decided if someone got the wrong impression, that was their own goddamned fault. She shouldn't be wary of looking nice when she went out because the male species was incapable of platonic friendships, nor should she be worried about coworkers, men and women, who were juvenile enough to infer that she must be sharing a bed with her boss because she decided to look nice at her own damn celebration.

Dressed up and on the road, Lucy had finally put the bad feelings out of her mind. Finally convinced herself that Raquel and Stephanie would show up, even though they hadn't responded to her text messages asking them what time they would arrive at Travis's house.

But the moment she pulled into the driveway, her heart sank to the pit of her stomach and alarm bells rang in her head.

The only vehicle present was Travis's Audi. The nagging feeling something was amiss had turned into a full-blown red flag. Still, rather than turn around, she parked the car in the driveway and debated her course of action. In the end, she'd looked at the clock and decided maybe she was simply the first to arrive. It was fifteen minutes prior to the start time Travis had told her. She cursed herself for being punctual, rather than one of those people who always showed up fashionably late. Besides, even if she wasn't early, it was entirely possible the other guests were running late. Most people didn't show up at the exact designated time for a party that wasn't their own. And of course there were always unforeseen circumstances to consider: car trouble, traffic, children. She needed to stop assuming the worst of every situation, which was something she'd been working on with her therapist. For too long she'd let the anxiety of what-ifs prevent her from living the life she wanted to live. Today, she would ignore the anxiety and on Monday afternoon, give her therapist a reason to be proud of her.

As that final thought on the matter crossed her mind, she exited her vehicle and made her way to the front porch. She wasn't going to let her brain's constant battles with itself ruin her life anymore.

Travis answered the door. He was clearly dressed to impress. Flashing a smile, he said, "Hello, Lucy, you look stunning."

She ignored the compliment. One thing she learned in her life about men was that they would always interpret politeness as a green light. "Hey, Travis, looks like I'm early," she said.

"Of course, you're always early, especially at the office. You've worked hard for this promotion. Frankly, it was long overdue, so I figured what better way to apologize for the delay than by celebrating this victory."

"Say, where is everyone? I haven't heard from Raquel

or Stephanie. I know it's still early, but do you know when they'll be here?"

"I'm not sure where they're at now, but when I spoke with Stephanie a little while ago, she'd said they were riding together and would be here shortly."

Lucy shot a look at the living room behind Travis. He caught the direction of her gaze and stepped aside, waving her in. "C'mon in. No need to wait outside for them to show up. I've ordered wings and pizza, and the driver should be here any minute. Hopefully we won't have to wait too long for them to start eating. I'm starving."

Lucy took a hesitant step into the house, chewing her bottom lip until she tasted blood, a nervous tic of hers.

Travis ushered her to the nearby closet where, at his insistence, she hung her jacket before being whisked away to his fancy, well-stocked bar.

Travis leaned backward against the bar top; elbows propped against it. "Why don't we have a glass of wine to celebrate," he said, a Cheshire cat grin plastered across his face, exposing his perfectly white teeth.

Lucy didn't want to drink, didn't feel comfortable alone with Travis, but she was already in the belly of the beast with no backup. As most women do, she learned long ago that any perceived slight against a man could lead to a sudden, violent retaliation.

And so, she opted to placate him; better to have a glass of wine and keep him happy than risk an unintentional provocation of his anger.

One glass of wine became two, and still none of the others had arrived. Lucy did her best to prolong it, sipping it like the proverbial fine wine, which to Travis's credit, was an accurate descriptor of the drink he'd handed her.

When at last she'd finished the astringent liquid, Travis was there to pour a third. But Lucy wanted no part of it, she could already feel the alcohol dulling her senses. She wiped her mouth, waving him off.

As feared, Travis became furious, shouting at her. He called her a cocktease, a bitch, a slut—every derogatory, shitty comment bestowed upon women by men faced with rejection.

Her heart hammered in her chest and the adrenaline flooding her fight-or-flight response managed to push the effects of the alcohol away. Lucy tried to grab her keys from the bowl atop the dining room countertop, but they were not where she'd placed them. Behind her, she heard a jingling noise.

She breathed heavily, panicking now. She turned around.

"Looking for something?" he asked, dangling the keys. The Cheshire smile was gone, replaced with a vulpine grin that remained in place as he stalked forward.

"Travis, I want to go home. Please give me my keys," Lucy said.

He slid the keys back into his pocket. "Sure, babe, I'll give you your keys. After you repay me for the promotion. You don't get to lead me on, day in and day out, parading around with your tits out and your ass on display. You wanted my attention; you got your promotion. Now, you're gonna get that tight little body over here and start earning it with your mouth. If you're a good girl, and you really do your best work, we're only gonna do this once. But you *are* gonna suck this dick, and I *am* gonna have sex with you tonight. When we're done, if I feel like you really gave it your all, you're gonna take the Plan B I bought for you, you're gonna drive home, and you're gonna forget about tonight. If you can't do that . . . Well, let's just say you won't have to worry about your job much longer. You won't have to worry about much of anything if you don't keep that pretty little mouth shut."

Travis grabbed Lucy by the waist and leaned in, pressing his lips against her closed mouth. She resisted at first, her heart hammering in her chest.

I can't believe this is happening to me.

His tongue pressed hard against her closed lips; she squeezed her own lips tight, unwilling to give in so easily.

An idea came to mind, rather than delay the inevitable, she opened her lips, granting the slimeball's tongue entry. It slithered its way in and she suppressed both the urge to vomit and the urge to bite his tongue off, to taste the blood as she ripped the muscle from his mouth. Instead, Lucy reciprocated the kiss. With one hand she reached out to his waist, pulling him closer. His hard bulge a heavy weight against her midsection as he moaned with lust. With her free hand, Lucy felt blindly behind her back, careful not to alert the would-be rapist. She felt his hands fumble at her jeans. She moaned in protest but Travis, ever the scumbag, could not tell the difference between lust and fear. Or maybe he just didn't care. A rapist didn't worry about the emotions of his prey.

As Lucy felt the button of her jeans come undone, her hand grasped what she was searching for—the ceramic bowl. She gripped it tight and swung the heavy object in a downward arc, connected with the side of Travis's head. He crumpled to the ground.

Lucy buttoned her pants and stepped over the prone body, blood leaking from his ear and the shredded flesh along the side of his face. Good, the fucker deserved it. She wouldn't be returning to work and Travis would have a nice memory of her for the rest of his life.

She ran to the door but stopped before exiting. Her keys! She turned and ran back to Travis, but he was already stirring. She reached down to grab the keys from his pocket before he fully came to, but his arm shot out and his hand clamped down on her wrist like a vise. She felt the small bones in her wrist moving, ready to snap.

"You bitch," he roared, "look what you did to my face!"

Lucy *did* look for a moment, admiring her handiwork. She saw the blood pouring from the torn side of his face, pulled her leg back, and punted his head like a football. His nose crunched and blood spurted out. Travis screamed in agony and writhed around on the floor. He was in pain, but still conscious. Rather than attempt to grab the keys again, Lucy decided to make a run for it.

She bolted out the front door and ran, never looking back, until she couldn't breathe and had no choice but to stop.

She wanted to keep going but her lungs ached, and she had a stitch in her side ready to take her out of commission. She needed to get farther away, but if she didn't listen to her body she'd collapse. Adrenaline and panic would only take her so far. She wouldn't stop, though, so she conceded to slow down and walk until she felt she could run again. She reached in her pocket for her phone to call for help but it wasn't there.

"Shit," she said, shaking her head in frustration. "I must have left it in my jacket." There was nothing she could do but keep walking. She couldn't turn around now.

The wind whipped and howled, carrying the scent of pine trees and lake water with it. The full moon shone high in the sky above her, but the tall pine trees prevented most of the light from bathing the road in its glow. Had it been this dark when she fled from Travis? Lucy didn't think so. The ever-encroaching darkness brought intrusive thoughts. Fears. Lucy had never been afraid of the dark, not even as a child, but as a grown woman, she was smart enough to fear the real-life monsters that lurked in the shadows.

With technology at your fingertips, you no longer had to watch the evening news to discover the latest tragedy. Every time you scrolled Facebook, or *X*, or any other social media platform, it seemed there was a new murder, a new kidnapping, a new shooting. And while Lake Budlong wasn't a hotbed of criminal activity, there had been murmurs of a serial killer active in the Southern New England area. Not whispers from the authorities of course, they didn't want to rile up the population, but when you really started looking into things, there were an awful lot of young women turning up missing and dead in both Rhode Island and Massachusetts over the past few years.

Her skin prickled, small hairs standing on end. Alone in the dark, her mind wouldn't stop gravitating toward the worst of humankind, working overtime to creep her the fuck out. She needed to get the hell back to civilization as soon as possible, lest she give herself an aneurism letting her mind spiral out of control. And even if there was no serial killer lurking in the woods, there was at least one lunatic in the area who may come looking for her, and she didn't want to be around if he did get a mind to track her down.

She didn't get much farther down the road before she

heard a vehicle approaching from behind her. She angled her path of travel closer to the tree line. People drove with their noses in their cell phones all day, every day, and she hadn't just escaped Travis only to be pancaked by a reckless driver. Unless of course the driver *was* Travis.

Speaking of her former boss, Lucy had gotten herself so worked up she began to wonder if she would have been better off giving Travis the blow job he expected. Not that she wanted to do it, but now she was so petrified for her life that *anything* seemed a step above her current situation. What if he *did* come looking for her. Surely after what she'd done to him he wouldn't stop at rape.

Enough. That's bullshit and I know it. He's a fucking creep, and I did the right thing smashing his face and getting the fuck out of there. Maybe next time I'll grab my phone before I run off, though. She chuckled to herself, despite her fear, or maybe because of it. The mind has a funny way of protecting itself from total collapse.

Behind her, the vehicle was now close enough to bathe the area with the bright glow of its headlights.

She stood a bit straighter, scared stiff. The sound of the tires on the road grew louder even as the roar of the vehicle's engine grew softer.

Please don't stop. Please keep going. Please don't stop. Please keep going. She repeated the words in her head, a mantra to manifest what she wanted to happen. What she *needed* to happen. It didn't matter who was in the vehicle. Whether it was Travis, or the serial killer that may or may not exist, or even a random passerby, she wanted nothing to do with them. Wanted nothing more than to walk her ass home and live her life in peace.

The noise behind stopped abruptly. The lights cut off

and she was in darkness once more. Lucy didn't know what to do. Run into the woods? Take off down the road? Both options were shit.

Fuck it, I've kicked one piece of shit's ass today, what's one mor? She talked herself up, mentally preparing for a fight.

"Hey, asshole, why don't you keep on driving. You won't be the first prick I give a beatdown to today," she yelled at the driver.

Lucy peered into the vehicle's windshield. It was too dark for her to see inside. She figured it had to be a man. A woman wouldn't do this to another woman.

Unless she was a psychopath.

But she knew the odds of that were highly unlikely. She couldn't recall, but she thought she read a statistic somewhere that claimed men were more than three times as likely to commit a violent crime than a woman. She thought that seemed a bit low, if she was being honest. Maybe those numbers would be in her favor tonight. Because even though she had successfully defended herself against a considerably larger man, she would feel much better about her odds going against someone her own size.

The vehicle's high beams flicked on, blinding Lucy. She shielded her eyes, but it was too late. The lights were far too bright, and she'd been looking straight at them when they'd turned on. She tried to turn her head and open her eyes but it was no use, she was blinded.

In the darkness, the sound of a car door opening and closing cut through the silence.

In the headlights, she could tell nothing about the vehicle. Couldn't make out its color, make, or model. As the driver stepped to the front, the headlights backlit them, but left Lucy unable to pick out any defining features. They were wearing what appeared to be a hoodie, cinched tight over their head. Further details eluded her.

Patting herself down, Lucy searched for anything in her pockets that she might be able to use as a weapon. The search came up empty, only finding a small, blue lighter. Didn't people say that if you made a fist with something inside, it made you punch harder? Lucy thought she could remember her father telling her that years ago. She squeezed her hand tight around the lighter, hoping it would be enough.

It had to be enough.

"That you, Travis?" Lucy asked. "You want some more?" She strode forward, displaying false bravado. She hoped she sounded intimidating, because she didn't feel intimidating at all.

The driver stepped toward her. She still couldn't see well, her eyes hadn't recovered from being blinded by the high beams, and the backlighting they cast over the figure left it cloaked in darkness. But she could see well enough now to discern that it was a man's frame. Despite her impaired vision, she was confident he wasn't Travis. This man was a good head taller than him.

The man let something long slip from inside his sleeve, catching it by the end. It was a mean, hard-looking thing. The realization that this was some stranger with a weapon ripped any sense of confidence from Lucy, false or otherwise. Who knew what this psychopath's deal was? She did an about-face and bolted. A sprinter off the block. She cursed herself for not running sooner. Stupid of her to think she was going to scare this person away. If she was caught now, it would be her own fault for not running as soon as the car approached her.

She felt the dirt crunching underfoot even as she heard the heavy steps of the man pursuing her. It didn't take long for Lucy to tire; she was still not recovered from her battle with Travis or her earlier flight from his house. Her heart hammered in her chest as the realization that she couldn't run much farther sank in. It was a horrible feeling, one that was impossible to force aside—knowing that your life depended on your body's ability to do something it didn't have the capability of doing.

Closer behind her, she could hear the man's breath now. Lucy clenched the lighter, turned around, and swung a wild fist but the man easily jumped back a step, throwing her off-balance. Just as she recovered, she saw a blur of motion out of the corner of her eye before the tire iron smashed against the side of her face, tearing the skin and shattering both her jaw and orbital bone. She felt a flash of pain, but only for an instant.

Then, blackness.

The man circled Lucy's motionless body, slipped the tire iron under his belt, and grabbed her by the underarms. He pulled her toward the vehicle, her heels carving a trail in the dirt road leading from where she'd been attacked, all the way back to the rear of her assailant's vehicle. With a grunt, he heaved her over his shoulder, then tossed her into the open trunk.

3

———————

The last few weeks of school passed by uneventfully, and before they knew it, the senior class of Budlong High walked the aisle, adorned in their green and white caps and gowns. Tommy, Joey, and Jackie, along with Tommy's girlfriend, Rowan, all members of the graduating class.

Now eighteen and finished with high school, Tommy, much like other young men and women his age, believed he had the world at his fingertips. And he did. The upcoming summer would be his last before college and he wanted to live it up. He knew things would never be the same again. Already, things were changing. Even within his own home. His father had started giving him a little more leeway—the same leeway Jackie had always gotten, now bestowed upon Tommy—as if graduating high school suddenly changed everything.

Maybe it did. Is this what it felt like to become a man?

Tommy never took any blackmail money from Joey after discovering his perverted deed. Rather than make a quick buck, he decided to enlist Jackie in a funnier prank. One that required her to plant a seed and nurture it. She'd spent the last few weeks getting closer to Joey, pretending to like him. Tonight, if all went well, they'd catch him on camera with his pants down—literally. What they would do with the evidence afterward was something they had yet to consider. One step at a time.

It would be smooth sailing from here on out. The toughest parts had already gone off without a hitch. Joey, with no clue as to what they had planned, had swiped the keys to his father's boat and Jackie had gotten alcohol from one of her friends. There was nothing left to do but enjoy themselves as they floated along Lake Budlong.

It had crossed Tommy's mind that maybe they were taking things a bit too far, but each time the thought popped into his head it was quickly dashed away by the image of Joey rubbing one out in his sister's closet. The fucking perv needed to be taught a lesson.

Sprawled out on the deck lounge chair, the summer breeze from the lake cooled the otherwise hot, evening air. It was unseasonably warm, and his pasty white flesh had turned red long ago from sun exposure. With youth on his side, Tommy never considered the long-term ramifications of poor decisions such as rawdogging the sun. It was so far down the list that his teenage mind couldn't comprehend such things as skin cancer.

He was eighteen. Invincible.

Across the deck, his girlfriend, Rowan, sprawled out on another chair, reading her Kindle. He'd bought her the new Colorsoft, a gift she absolutely adored. She always had her face buried in it. On the chair next to Rowan, Jackie sat on Joey's lap, whispering something in his ear.

Rowan looked over the top of the Kindle and giggled. They were all still high from the joint they'd smoked. Tommy wasn't sure what she was laughing about. Something in the book? Had she overheard Jackie and Joey? Either way, her laugh was infectious and every time Tommy heard it, his heart skipped a beat. He basked in the glow of the moment. Happy. At ease. He loved Rowan, or at least what constituted love at their age. He didn't know if it was true love. He supposed it wasn't, but he knew that he loved the way she made him feel. Regardless, they would soon be off to college, and while part of him wanted to be with her always, there was another part of him that relished the opportunity to meet new people. That part of him chirped endlessly in the back of his mind, and often ruined moments such as this. For that reason, when thoughts of love crossed his mind, he told himself it was more about how he felt with her than truly loving her. Otherwise, why would his mind wander? Tonight, he pushed those thoughts aside. Whatever the future held was just that—the future. But for now, they were here and he wanted to relish the moment.

Jackie moaned, a sound that normally would have gotten his teenage body rock hard, but coming from his sister there was no such effect. Instead, his stomach roiled with disgust. He shot a look that could kill across the deck. Her acting skills were a bit *too* good for his liking. The plan was to make Joey *think* she wanted to fuck him, not to actually do it. When he'd first told her about the incident, she was livid, and had even threatened to kill him. But Tommy eventually calmed her down, convinced her there was something better than murder. Revenge. They would embarrass him, film it, and maybe even post the footage online for all of their recently graduated classmates to see. He knew it sounded fucked-up. And really, it was. But Joey was a good sport, he'd get over it.

Consider the online humiliation a parting gift for the graduates of Budlong High before they were off to college. Before life would eventually chew them up and spit them out.

Until the moment she'd made that disgusting sound, he was satisfied with how their plan had turned out. Jackie was a beautiful young woman, and Joey was a teenager full of testosterone and lack of self-control. Wrapping him around her finger was a task that required little effort. Jackie jumped headfirst into the plan, talking to Joey every day. They grew thick as thieves, Joey none the wiser.

Reflecting on the past few weeks, Tommy thought it amazing how quickly a woman could work her magic, especially on a fool like Joey who no doubt did most of his thinking with the head between his legs rather than the one between his shoulders.

They continued flirting, Tommy growing more uncomfortable as he looked on, sickened by the thought of his sister acting like a grown woman, even though that had been the plan all along. He never considered how vomit-inducing it would be to witness it in person. She deserved an Oscar for the act she was putting on because if Tommy didn't know any better, he'd swear they were moments away from slapping skin below deck.

Having a twin sister was tough. Having an attractive twin sister was worse. There was no end to the jokes he was forced to endure. Every Tom, Dick, and Harry at school thought they were funny, making little comments about Jackie. But Tommy didn't see the humor in it. Most days he simply let it slide. But there had been one incident that had gone too far. One of Budlong's star football players made an especially vulgar comment about losing No Nut November to a wet dream about Jackie.

When he'd heard it, Tommy snapped. Then surprised himself when the looping punch landed square on the prick's jaw, knocking him out cold. It was a lucky one, that punch. If it had been a legit fight and not a sucker punch, he might not have landed it. Certainly wouldn't have hit the dumb jock's reset button with it. But it *did* land, and with that knockout punch, people had learned to keep Jackie's name out of their mouths.

At least around Tommy.

Rowan coughed, grabbing Tommy's attention. She wore oversized sunglasses despite the sun having set long ago. She lifted them and gave Tommy a wink. "Time to get this show on the road," the gesture said.

Tommy gave a subtle nod in response. It wouldn't have mattered. Judging by the way Joey had to constantly rearrange his shorts, it was a safe assumption that he paid no mind to anyone else on the boat aside from Jackie.

Tommy stood up and stretched. "All right, guys, Rowan and I are gonna head below deck. Don't do anything crazy up here," he said. As the words left his mouth he realized he meant them. Jackie might have agreed to be in on the gag, but clearly somewhere along the line things had gotten serious between the two of them. Would she still do her part? Tommy hoped so.

He reached for Rowan's hand, their fingers interlocking. He shivered at her touch every time, like it was the first time.

They made their way below deck where there were two

small bedrooms, one on each side. Joey's dad had plenty of money to spare on luxuries such as this boat. Joey told them Mr. Harrison had given them permission to take the boat out on the lake, but Tommy knew the truth—Joey hadn't asked, simply taken the keys. Mr. Harrison was rarely home, frequently on business trips that took him out of state. According to Joey, he expected his father to be out of town for a few more days, at least.

They shut the door to the small bedroom on the right side and entered the open door to the other bedroom. Calling them bedrooms was a bit generous. The two rooms were originally open space that had been partitioned off. Mr. Harrison had plenty of money, but it wasn't like they were on some massive luxury craft. Within the "master bedroom," there was a tiny section closed off from the rest. A mini closet. Tommy squeezed his way inside and Rowan attempted to follow but there wasn't enough room.

"I'll just slide under the bed," Rowan said. "At least that way I can still hear everything. I don't know if I want to see what's gonna happen anyway."

"Nothing is going to happen; Jackie wouldn't do anything with him."

"From where I was sitting, it seemed like she wanted to do a lot with him. Sounded like it too."

Tommy's face flushed red. "Just hide before they get in here."

Rowan smiled and shimmied under the bed. Tommy enjoyed the view. When Rowan was in position, he pulled his phone from his pocket and opened the camera app, switching it to video. He adjusted the settings to record in 4K with 60FPS. Not only was it going to be a good show, it was going to be excellent quality. Tommy wanted to make sure there was no question of who was in the video.

He finished setting up not a moment too soon. Jackie entered the room with Joey in tow. Tommy held the phone up, aiming the lens through the slats in the door. The two of them walked all the way around to the other side of the bed before sitting down next to each other. Not a word passed between them before they started making out. Jackie guided one of Joey's hands to her breast. He did nothing at first, simply held it there, as if he was unsure what to do. After a few moments, he began awkwardly fondling her chest like he was kneading dough. The sight of his best friend groping his sister's tits sent Tommy's blood pressure through the roof, but he kept quiet and filmed. Even when Jackie reached down and stuck her hand in Joey's shorts, working his penis, Tommy somehow managed to not vomit.

Jackie stood up, reached her hand behind her back, and pulled the tie on her bikini top loose. It slid to the floor, landing right in front of Rowan. Tommy thanked God her back was to him; he didn't need that kind of trauma in his life. From his vantage point he could see Rowan place her hand over her mouth. Whether she was holding in a gasp or a laugh, Tommy was unsure.

Joey stood, but Jackie pushed him down. "Lie on your back," she said.

Joey did as he was told and Jackie grabbed his swim trunks where they ended at the knees and pulled. His shorts flew down to his ankles and his three-and-a-half-inch soldier stood at attention. Tommy snorted and quickly covered his mouth.

"What was that?" Joey asked.

"I didn't hear anything." Jackie replied.

Shit, shit, shit, Tommy cursed himself.

"No, I heard something," Joey insisted.

Jackie dropped to her knees and grabbed Joey's stiff cock with her first three fingers, there wasn't much real estate for her entire hand, despite the fact that they were small. Up and down her hand went before she leaned forward and placed her mouth over his mini helmet.

Tommy had seen enough of that. He burst from the closet and shouted, "Surprise!"

Jackie shot up. "What the fuck?!" she exclaimed, feigning shock.

The surprise intrusion, along with the fact that his cock had been in Jackie's mouth, even if for only a moment, sent Joey over the edge. His body spasmed as arcing ropes of jizz pumped from the tip of his dick. The first spurt splattered against Jackie's cheek, the second, across her bare breasts.

"Eww, are you fucking kidding me?" Jackie screamed.

Tommy laughed, circling around to catch everything. "This turned out even better than I hoped. Not only did we get your baby dick on camera, but the whole world is gonna know you're a two pump chump!" He laughed at his own joke, panning the camera down to Joey's groin. "Then again, calling you a two pump chump is a bit more credit than you deserve, huh?"

"What the hell is going on here? Jackie? What is this?" Joey asked, panic evident in his voice.

Rowan crawled out from underneath the bed on the side opposite everyone else. She crossed the room and pushed Tommy's hand down. Despite having been in on the shenanigans, she had a look of concern on her face. "Enough," she said.

"Is it? We're just having fun, right, Joey? Just a little payback for what you did in my sister's room," Tommy said.

"You told me you weren't gonna say anything," Joey said. He looked at Jackie, "You knew? For how long?"

Jackie bowed her head, seemingly ashamed of what she'd done.

What the hell is wrong with them? Tommy thought. *They all thought the idea was great a few weeks ago, now they've got cold feet?*

Jackie looked at Joey once more. She must have seen something in his eyes, hurt, maybe. Or maybe she really had begun to fall for him. Whatever the reason, she looked at her brother, shielding her breasts with her arm, and said, "Just knock it off. It isn't funny anymore."

"So you *were* in on it," Joey said. "All this time I thought you really liked me." A lone tear ran down his cheek. "Fuck all of you!" he shouted, venom and hurt evident in his voice as he turned around and ran.

Tommy couldn't help but laugh as he watched his friend stumble awkwardly in a half run-half trot. He tripped, fell on the floor, then pulled his shorts up and left.

"Joey, wait," Jackie called after him. But he was already gone. "We fucked up," she said, turning toward her brother.

Tommy's eyes fell on his sister's breasts. They glistened in spots where the cum had splattered against her skin. He looked away quickly, he may be a horndog, but his sister's tits weren't a source of arousal for him. He grabbed a towel from the closet and tossed it at her, while still keeping his eyes trained in the opposite direction. "Clean yourself up and put your damn top on, for Christ's sake."

Jackie's face blushed as she turned around and wiped herself off. She picked her bikini top up and tied it back in place. "Let's go fix this, please, Tommy." She shook her head. "I know we agreed to prank him, but I never really considered what we were doing. It's too much. We didn't think this through."

"It's too much because you fell for the fucking guy. You weren't supposed to suck him off, you were supposed to get him naked."

"I don't have to explain shit to you. Don't be such a piece of shit your whole life. He's your best friend. Show some empathy."

"Empathy? He's a fucking pervert."

Rowan spoke up, "Says the guy filming his sister and his best friend so he can upload it to social media. Pretty sure voyeurism is illegal. You're officially a sex offender, buddy."

"Really? Now you? Fine, go talk to him. Maybe we can calm him down, but I still think we should bust his balls some more."

"What do we even say to smooth over something like this?" Rowan asked.

"I don't know. Maybe Jackie could give him another blowie. He seemed to have really liked the first one," Tommy said, laughing.

Jackie shook her head. "You're a pig. Fucking disgusting."

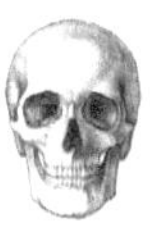

On the deck, the temperature had dropped a bit. Joey stood against the railing, staring off into space. The three of them emerged from below deck, Jackie in the lead. She called out, "Joey, can we please talk? I owe you an apology."

Joey stood still for a few moments. Long enough that Jackie opened her mouth to repeat herself, but Joey spun around and replied, "You're sorry? You led me on all night long. No, fuck that, you led me on for *weeks*. You made me feel like we had something between us, only to find out that your creep, sick fuck of a brother, who I thought was my best friend, was hiding in a closet filming me? Filming *us?* That's sick, and you're a fucking skank."

Tommy spoke up, "Hey man, that's my—"

Jackie cut her brother off, "Joey, I understand why you're upset, you have every right to be. Tommy told me about what happened in my room, and at first we thought a little prank would be funny. When I started texting you, it *was* fake. In the beginning. But I really *do* like you. It wasn't all fake, it just started out that way. The more we talked, the more I liked you. And as this evening went along, everything I did, I did because I wanted to."

Joey shook his head. "Because you're a slut, that's why you did it. You're a slut."

The comment hit her right in the heart. She knew she wasn't a slut, but that was the first time someone had called her that and it made her feel lower than she'd ever felt before, made her question if what she had done to Joey *had* been slutty.

Tommy, clearly having heard enough, strode across the deck and stood nose to nose with Joey. "Listen, asshole, call my sister a slut, or any other shitty name again and we're going to have a fucking problem here. She said she was sorry, and I was getting ready to do the same. Maybe we took it overboard, but you were being a perv. I wanted to teach you a lesson. It's done now."

Jackie, still hurt from what Joey had called her, stepped between the two boys. It had gone on too long and had gone much too far. She didn't want her brother and his best friend fighting over her, even if what Joey said was fucked-up. She spread her arms out, trying to separate the two but Joey pushed her aside with a swat. Pain flashed where his hand had slapped her across the chest and she fell flat on her ass, skidding across the deck.

The moment Jackie hit the floor Tommy shoved Joey, who stumbled backward on the slippery deck. Tommy took advantage of Joey's loss of balance. He stepped forward and threw a straight, right-handed punch before Joey could recover. The sound of bone on bone contact was loud enough to be heard over Jackie crying. Tommy's fist gnashed Joey's teeth together with an audible *click*. A white blur flew across the night sky, sailing over the deck into the lake–Joey's tooth.

"Stop it!" Jackie screamed.

Joey regained his footing and cocked his arm back, but he'd never been in a fight in his life and had no defense for the follow-up punch that landed on the side of his jaw. He scrambled to keep his footing, his feet appearing to run in place like a cartoon character slipping on a banana peel.

The comical sight of Joey slipping in stark contrast to the severity of the events transpiring almost forced laughter out of Jackie, which died in her throat as Joey's head smacked the deck with a sickening *crack*. His unconscious body slid across the slippery deck, under the railing, and into the water, leaving a bloody snail trail behind.

Jackie screamed. A high-pitched wail that would make any scream queen jealous.

Rowan watched on, silent. Her face frozen in a rictus of terror.

Tommy was also frozen in place, though his face had a vacant look plastered across it, as if he was shocked that the result of their little scuffle had been so disastrous.

Finally, Rowan screamed, "Tommy, don't just fucking stand there, do something!"

Tommy didn't react to her plea. Not because he was shocked, but because he was scared to death. He couldn't swim, and after a close call in the lake as a child, he'd never made an attempt to learn or get back in the water. The boat was the closest he had come to a body of water in years.

Jackie knew her brother's fear, knew there was no hope of him helping, so she sprang into action. "Tommy, snap the fuck out of it and throw the life preserver in the water," she said, taking charge of the situation.

Without saying another word, Jackie jumped over the railing, splashing into the dark water below. Her actions so quick, so unexpected that neither Tommy nor Rowan could have stopped her if they tried.

The water was cold, piercing icicles through her skin. Though she'd done the penguin challenge many times before, running into the freezing ocean in the middle of the winter, it didn't make this venture into the water suck any less. The previous experience simply enabled her to grasp onto a mind-over-matter mentality. She had to do this. If she couldn't push through the pain of the cold lake, Joey was as good as dead.

Even if she could, he might already be dead. He'd taken a hard fall. But at least if she could get to him, he might stand a chance.

Swimming beneath the surface, her mind ran in circles. *Is the water cold enough to give me hypothermia? Did the blow to Joey's head kill him? Or is he unconscious, taking water into his lungs as he sinks like a stone to the bottom of the lake? How deep is the lake?*

Jackie felt her heart hammering in her chest, a mixture of adrenaline and panic gripping her. She tried to calm herself, slow her heart rate. The more she kept herself under control, the more time she would be able to spend below the surface, searching for Joey. She knew every second counted.

Jackie swam until her lungs burned. She surfaced, took a deep breath, and went below once more. It was dark down there, she could see, but not much more than an arm's length in front of her. Once more, her panic-induced thoughts made it difficult for her to stay calm. What if she swam too far and couldn't get back to the boat, she'd already exerted herself greatly the first time she'd gone under. Would she be able to make it to the life preserver if she taxed herself too much?

It didn't matter. Joey was down there because of her. She had to try. She owed him that much. Jackie swam around, but the soft glow of the moon did little to help visibility below the surface. It was no use; she needed a light.

A light, she thought. If only she had stopped to think for a moment before diving into the lake, she might already have what she needed. In the back of her mind, Jackie worried her hasty decision would be the final nail in Joey's coffin.

Breaking the surface once more, Jackie sucked wind, her entire body aching, muscles burning from lactic acid buildup and oxygen deprivation. She looked around, searching for the boat. It was well within a distance she normally would have been able to swim, but she was exhausted, her gas tank spent. *I can't swim that far,* she thought. Panicking, she flailed her arms and kicked her feet wildly.

"Jackie, hold on!" Tommy yelled.

Darkness encroached upon her vision. She could see the bright white beacon of the boat, but couldn't make out her brother. A splash hit the water to her left. Her flailing arm found the life preserver and she hooked her arms around it.

Tommy pulled the rope attached to the device, the tendons in his neck and veins in his arms bulging as each pull of the rope brought his sister closer to safety.

Jackie coughed and spat out water. "I couldn't find him, it's too dark down there." She kicked her legs as she held onto the flotation device, but her attempts were too weak to be of any real assistance to her brother's rescue efforts.

The device had finally reached the boat, and Jackie grasped for the ladder, but was too weak to pull herself up. Tommy jumped in, never mind that he couldn't swim and was terrified of the water. With a splash, he landed next to his sister, grabbing the ladder with one hand and wrapping his other arm around Jackie's waist.

"We're right here," he said. "Just pull yourself up a little bit and I can push you the rest of the way. I just need you to do a little bit of the work."

Jackie tried to focus all her remaining energy on pulling herself up. She knew her brother had to be panicking, even if he was doing a good job hiding it. Below her, she felt Tommy shoving her to safety. Jackie pulled up, using the combined strength of her brother's push with what little effort she could muster. Slowly, after what felt like ages, she reached the top of the ladder, rolled over the top of it, and with Rowan's help, made it onto the deck.

Jackie remained flat on her back, her vision swimming while her chest heaved, sucking in oxygen.

Rowan helped pull Tommy onto the deck, though he didn't need her assistance.

Jackie's lungs and muscles ached, burned as if they were on fire. But as Rowan and Tommy approached her, she shot up as if hit with another burst of adrenaline. "Joey!" she croaked, coughing harsh barks that stung her throat as she scrambled unsteadily to her feet. She took one step before a wave of coughing took over, her body spasming. A stream of water and snot spewed from her mouth and nose.

Tommy placed his hand between her shoulders as she ejected the lake water from her body. "Jackie, you tried your best."

She wiped the stringy liquid from her face. "I tried my best? He's still down there, and I couldn't fucking save him Tommy. He's down there because of our actions. If I would have grabbed one of the waterproof lights first, he might be up here with us. But I didn't, and now he's nowhere to be found."

"So, what do we do?" Tommy asked, looking at both Rowan and Jackie for guidance.

"I already called the cops when you were looking for him. There's nothing else we can do," Rowan said.

"Speaking of phones," Tommy said, patting his shorts. He plunged his hands into his pockets and pulled them inside out, coming up empty-handed. "I have no idea where mine is. I must have dropped it when we got into the argument."

"You sure it's not below deck?" Jackie asked.

Tommy's face went red for a moment. "No, I was filming when we got up here," he admitted, the embarrassment in his voice evident.

"You really are something else. Forget about your fucking phone. Your best friend is still out there somewhere," Jackie chided.

"You know what? You're right, but there's no way we're going to be able to get to him. You tried," Tommy said, his voice no longer betraying his shame, but rather taking on a steely quality. "The cops are on their way right now; we need to get our facts straight before they get here."

"What do you mean get our facts straight?" Jackie asked. "You guys got into a fight, and he fell in the water. It was an accident."

Jackie felt her brother's vise-like grip as he snatched her by the wrist, squeezing her. His nails dug into her, little crescents of blood appearing where they pierced the flesh. "Yeah Jackie, but you know what they call that?

Manslaughter. I accidently caused his death; people go to jail for manslaughter. And what do you think is going to happen to you? You'll be an accessory to the crime for your part of the prank, and I don't think it's a stretch for Joey's dad to make that happen. The fucking guy is rich, and he knows everyone in town."

"Why would they arrest anyone? It was an accident," Jackie repeated.

"Money, that's why. Because if *someone* doesn't go down for this, Mr. Harrison has more than enough money to make hell for the lives of the political appointees of this Podunk town. You don't think the chief of police likes his job? I'm not risking it. Joey's dead and we can't take it back. But that doesn't change the fact that it was an accident. Do you want to see me go to prison for defending my sister? Because that isn't going to bring him back. And can you imagine what it would do to Mom and Dad?"

Jackie nodded her head. Tommy was right. She knew it, but she didn't like it. This was a side of her brother she'd never seen before. It was like he flipped a mental switch and no longer cared about his friend drowning. He was too worried about self-preservation. But she kept her thoughts to herself and her mouth shut as Tommy spun the story the three of them would tell the police officers when they arrived on scene.

In the distance, sirens could be heard.

4

———

P olice sirens sliced through the otherwise calm ambience of Lake Budlong, but the piercing noise could not breach the suffocating water.

At the bottom of the lake, Joey Harrison was motionless. Blood leaked from the back of his skull, his life essence mixing with the freshwater, his being becoming one with nature.

From a fissure in the ground, the result of recent seismic activity, black ooze seeped forth. It had been trapped beneath the earth's surface for centuries, but no more. It moved in stops and starts, like a Claymation movie below the surface. The ooze moved with a purpose, the oily black substance inching ever closer to Joey's corpse.

A school of tiny fish swam by, and a black tendril shot forth from the ooze, spearing one of the creatures and reeling it into its mass, adsorbing the fish while the rest of its companions darted away from the newly introduced predator. A predator that had no equal in any of the earth's biomes.

The ooze crept along the bottom of the lake, attacking and combining with any life unfortunate enough to pass too closely.

At Joey's feet now, the ooze shot forth, latching onto his leg. It spread itself thin, stretching like taffy, working its way along Joey's entire body until the only part not covered in the alien substance was his head. A length of ooze stretched forward farther, flitting at Joey's nose like a snake's tongue. It pulled back momentarily before splitting in two and shooting up each of Joey's nostrils. The dead teen's entire body was now covered from head to toe, his insides soon to follow.

It worked its way throughout the entire body, invading and consuming.

5

———

Tommy ran his hands up and down his crossed arms, the friction doing little to warm him up. Wearing only his swim trunks, he sat in the steel chair, which was bolted to the ground in front of a steel table, also bolted to the ground. The table was smack-dab in the middle of the drab interview room of the Budlong Police Department. Between the temperature of the room, and the BPD's unwillingness to give Tommy a shirt to wear, it didn't take a genius to deduce that the detectives were intentionally making him uncomfortable. He'd seen more than enough television procedurals to spot the tactic.

No dummy, Tommy knew they suspected foul play. The scratches on his knuckles were enough to lead detectives to believe there had been a scuffle, but they had no concrete evidence, which is why they were trying to get him to crack. Their only concern was closing a case; if they could get him to self-incriminate, it would eliminate countless man-hours on investigation and paperwork. Well, they weren't getting shit out of Tommy without a lawyer. These Podunk pigs could try all they wanted to break him, but the Ross family kept a decent attorney on retainer. All he had to do was wait for the man to arrive and they'd be good to go, so long as Jackie and Rowan didn't squeal. He didn't think they would, but who could say? Jackie was blood, yes, and at any other time he would have said there was no way in hell she would give up her twin, but after the way she behaved tonight, he wasn't so sure. Rowan was another toss-up. She was his girlfriend, but they were young and had their entire lives ahead of them. Tommy wasn't naive enough to believe she'd be willing to risk that future for her high school boyfriend. She may stay the course for now, but if the detectives were determined to put the squeeze on them, Tommy knew it would only be a matter of time before she folded.

He tapped his foot nervously, the evening's events playing through his mind like a movie stuck on a loop. Joey running off with his bare ass cheeks hanging out. The three of them following. The fight. Jackie in the water. Jackie back on the boat. Tommy drilling the story they were to run with into their heads, over and over and over until they were able to recite it without a second thought. In the end, the story amounted to the simplest explanation possible: Joey had too much to drink, the deck was wet, he slipped and fell. No need to add anything more to the equation, doing so would only make it easier for someone to slip up.

But there had been one problem with Tommy's story, something he hadn't realized until Jackie brought it to his attention. At some point, authorities would drag the lake and recover Joey's body. When that happened, it wasn't going to take a coroner to point out injuries to Joey's face that were inconsistent with their story.

Rather than take a chance, they decided on a story that made even Tommy sick to his stomach. Joey didn't have an accident. Joey was a predator. He'd had too much to drink, put the moves on Jackie. Jackie rejected him, and being a drunken eighteen-year-old rich kid, he hadn't taken the rejection well. At that point, Joey had gotten handsy with Jackie. Tommy heard the commotion, went above deck, and intervened. A simple accident. The story was shoddy, the teens all knew it, and if the way BPD treated Tommy was an indication, they knew it too.

Tommy's thoughts were interrupted when the door to the interview room swung open, crashing against the wall. Robert Igliozzi, the Ross family attorney, stormed into the room. Igliozzi was a tall man who looked as if he would be at home playing in a Scorsese movie. He wore his dark black hair swept back, held in place with too much product. His suit, expensive and freshly pressed, was immaculately tailored to his fit body. Tommy had only met the man once before, when his mother had been rear-ended by a drunk driver. His father had hired Igliozzi that evening after they'd left the hospital. Tommy recalled his dad telling him on the car ride home that the man was a "pitbull" in the courtroom, and the guy who hit Mrs. Ross would be eating Ramen noodles for the rest of his miserable life when they were through with him.

Tommy couldn't speak for the accuracy of the statement, but he assumed it had some truth to it, considering the size of the settlement check they'd received from the accident. If Igliozzi was half as good at criminal defense as civil cases ,then Tommy didn't have much to worry about.

Trailing behind Igliozzi, his face beet red, was Detective Carlisle. Carlisle looked like steam might pour from his ears at any second. He huffed and puffed like a scolded child and stood in the corner of the room, his arms crossed over his chest, one foot up, firmly planted against the wall.

Igliozzi broke the silence, clearing his throat, drawing all eyes to him. Shavings to a magnet. He spoke directly to Tommy, ignoring the detective. "Tommy, you are free to go. You will not hear from the detectives any further unless I am present. If, for some reason, they contact you, you will say nothing to them aside from requesting my presence. The good Samaritan in you may wish to answer their questions," he said, nodding at Carlisle, "but I can assure you it is never in anyone's best interest. As you may have ascertained by the way this interview was conducted, the BPD has no interest other than assigning blame to a tragedy. A tragedy which they intend on using to spin you as a murderer."

Tommy may have made a stupid mistake, but he was by no means a stupid person. He kept his mouth shut and stood, walking out of the room as fast as his legs could carry him. As he passed Carlisle, the detective placed a hand on his shoulder. "Be seeing you around, kid."

Igliozzi's head snapped in Carlisle's direction. "No, you won't be seeing him, detective. If I so much as catch wind of you driving down this young man's street, I'll have your badge so fucking fast your head will spin. I've got a lot of dirt on you, Carlisle. Would be a shame if certain things were to get out. How would that gold-digging wife of yours react? I've got a feeling the paperwork would be drawn up the same day and the next night she'd be sucking your partner's cock. Someone's gotta keep the bed warm, right? And who better than your best friend to take care of your wife when you can't?"

Tommy had never seen anyone's face turn that shade of red before. He kept moving, not wanting to be around if Carlisle lost his cool.

Suddenly, Tommy wasn't so worried about the Budlong Police Department.

6

———

Lucy opened her eyes and saw nothing but darkness. Her head pounded and her face felt every bit as mangled as it was. She tried to scream, but the pain in her jaw exploded, sending bright white flashes through her vision. She sobbed quietly, trying not to move her jaw.

Unable to sit up or move any of her extremities, Lucy realized she was strapped to something, and the memory of the events that led her to this moment hit her like a ton of bricks. She struggled against the restraints, but it was no use. They were too tight, even her head was held in place by something across her forehead. This time Lucy was able to scream, despite the searing pain shooting through her jaw. The intensity of the pain was unlike anything she'd ever felt before, causing her to vomit. Chunks of regurgitated food erupted from her mouth, some of it spilling over the side of her face, much of it not coming out with enough force to clear her mouth.

Lucy gagged, not from the horrible stench, but because she was choking on her own vomit. Her life flashed before her eyes as she asphyxiated, unable to clear her airway. She tried swallowing the vile stomach eruption, but it was no use. Lucy's vision swam, darkening at the corners. With luck, she'd die like an animal choking on her own vomit, rather than whatever the fiend who'd assaulted her had in store for her.

Teetering on the verge of unconsciousness, she didn't hear the door slam open and barely noticed the lights flick on. She'd simply thought what she was seeing was literally the light at the end of the tunnel. Her time to die. Maybe heaven existed and this was Jesus calling her home.

She felt something enter her mouth, holding it open, and then felt something scraping along the back of her throat before scooping toward her mouth. Oxygen rushed into her lungs. She gleefully sucked down the air. It was easy to wish for death when you were scared; it was another thing entirely to welcome it when you were looking it straight in the eyes.

Maybe she wasn't quite ready to die.

Lucy tried to look around, but could only move one eye, the other was swollen shut. The undamaged eye could see nothing but a blinding light. Barely detectable under the scent of vomit, she smelled the faint aroma of mildew. It made her think she was locked away somewhere her captor had little fear of being discovered, and that unlocked a deeper fear within her.

A head poked in front of her limited field of vision; a man she'd never seen before.

"Be careful now, we can't have you choking to death. That won't do at all," he said. He dug in his pocket, pulled something out. Lucy felt a rough cloth forced into her open mouth. Unbearable pain shot through her broken jaw, but with her mouth stuffed she was unable to scream.

The man grabbed one of Lucy's hands, pulling the pinky finger away from the ring finger. He held up a gleaming metal instrument, waving it slowly in front of her. Light glinted off the terrifying tool. "Bone shears, darling. Have you ever seen them before? They work wonders."

A moment of pressure turned to searing hot pain as the shears cut through her skin. Somehow the pain grew more intense as the shears stopped in place for a moment, stuck against bone. She heard the man grunt and then her pinky was gone, cut off just below the middle knuckle. The severed length hit the floor with a barely audible *plop*. Blood squirted from the wound like a practical effects prop, painting the dusty floor crimson.

Despite the broken jaw, despite the rag, she screamed. The gag muffled the sound enough that even if they weren't in a secluded area, nobody could have possibly heard unless they were standing next to her. Still, the screams must have been louder than her captor wanted because he shoved the rag deeper into her mouth. She breathed through her nose, trying not to gag on the rag, but the tip of the cloth was hitting the back of her throat and made her feel like she was choking.

The man disappeared from view for a moment before reappearing, holding her severed pinky over his lips in a shushing gesture. He laughed and placed the finger in a polished wooden box, which he placed somewhere off to the side and returned with a portable torch. Lucy thrashed as much as the restraints allowed, which wasn't much at all. Her muscles and tendons, once coiled serpents, lashing out, struggling for freedom.

The struggle was for naught. She pissed herself as the flame charred her pinky nub. The mind-numbing pain and scent of burning flesh sent her into the abyss once more, mercifully.

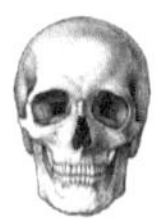

With the wound seeping, no longer squirting, the man applied an ointment to a gauze bandage and wrapped the digit. She was a gift, placed in his path. It was meant to be, and he would not let his plaything die until he was ready to give her the sweet release. It came at his will, nobody else's.

The man wheeled the small table into the corner of the room in the decrepit cabin. Far enough away from where his plaything was strapped down, just in case she somehow got a hand loose.

He watched her for a few minutes as she lay on his table. Unconscious. Waiting to die. Waiting for his gift.

They all awaited his gift.

His phone vibrated against his leg, the noise loud enough to pull him from his trance. He grabbed the phone and was about to hit the ignore button, but before he had the chance, the man noticed the caller ID.

Budlong Police Department, it read.

No. They couldn't have discovered my secret. They wouldn't call, would they? No. Certainly not. There would be a court order for a warrant, a SWAT team ready to unleash a volley of AR15 rounds. Blood and brains everywhere.

His mind ran circles wondering what reason the police would have to call him. "I'll be back soon, darling," the man whispered. He exited the room and placed the phone to his ear.

7

The smell of bleach stung Joey Harrison Sr.'s nostrils as he scrubbed the blood from the deck of his boat.

His son's blood.

He washed the stains away, the last part of Joey that remained. The only part that had been discovered. The Budlong Police Department had spent days dragging the lake for any signs of Joey, canvassing the few residents who lived along the lake. There weren't many left. Most of the cabins were owned by some company that had been sued years ago after a Marine veteran went crazy and killed all his buddies. The company, and the non-profit organization they'd rented it out to, had both been sued into bankruptcy. The few cabins not owned by the private company were mostly vacation homes, owned by families who rarely made the trip to Lake Budlong. It wasn't exactly a vacation hotspot.

When the company went under, Joey Harrison Sr. bought most of the cabins and proceeded to demolish them. He didn't like having neighbors. In the summertime, he dealt with beachgoers and boaters, but aside from that he had much of the lake, the woods, and the remaining buildings to himself. He'd tried purchasing the cabins owned by vacationers, and even though they rarely used them, many of the owners refused to sell. Fine by him. He was at least thankful that most of them were rarely occupied. With companies like Airbnb, he worried that would soon change. Was surprised it hadn't already.

He didn't like company.

His son, Joey Harrison Jr., dead at eighteen. The boy had only just become a man, only just walked across the stage. Now, he was gone. Snuffed from the world. He'd never go to college, never get married. No grandchildren for Mr. Harrison.

Dead at eighteen. Dead by way of his best friend's own hands. It stunk like shit, even the lead detective had admitted as much. But the Ross family had hired one hell of a good lawyer and the story the kids were running with painted Joey like some sort of alcoholic rapist. The most they were going to get was a manslaughter charge, and if Jackie played the jury well enough in court, really played up the brother as her savior angle, not only would the jury not convict, they would end up smearing Joey's name and reputation.

Smearing my *name and reputation,* he thought.

Mr. Harrison had the money and resources to make the Ross Family attorney look like a public defender, but considered his other options. Options that were far more appealing to him.

He gripped the mop handle until his knuckles were white. There had to be some way, some sort of evidence.

Joey couldn't have done what Jackie claimed, could he? He wanted to be sure before he made a rash decision.

Mr. Harrison thought about his own past, his own life. *Yeah, he sure could. But* did *he?* That was the question he needed to answer. When he had his answers, he would decide how to proceed.

With the last traces of his son wiped clean from the deck, Mr. Harrison tore down the crime scene tape, scrunched it up, and tossed it at the garbage can he'd set up. It hit the rim and rolled onto the deck, underneath one of the chairs. He got down on his hands and knees and reached for the tape.

There was something underneath the chair.

He pulled out a black phone case. The case featured an Orlando Magic logo printed across the back. Definitely not Joey's, he was a die-hard Celtics fan. He flipped the phone over and tapped the screen, but it didn't respond. He held the button on the side of the phone, and for a moment, a battery charging icon lit up the screen before going black once more.

The phone must belong to a friend of Joey's. Could it be Tommy's? It was impossible to say for sure, but clearly the Budlong Police Department was incapable of sweeping a crime scene for evidence. No wonder they couldn't find Joey's body in the lake. Maybe he'd take a ride by the Ross home later, see if anyone knew who the phone belonged to. Although it struck him a bit odd that nobody had come forth to reclaim the phone. This one had a location tracker, no doubt. There had to be a reason that whoever it belonged to hadn't come to retrieve their phone.

Mr. Harrison pondered the potential implications of

that. *Maybe I'll hold off on locating the owner,* he thought as he slid the phone into his pocket. He'd be able to hack the phone easily enough. With money, everything was easy.

His only son, dead at eighteen. Without Joey, Mr. Harrison had nothing left to lose.

Nothing to restrain him. No reason to be careful . . .

8

———

Things had been tough since Joey's death. Every day, despite what Mr. Igliozzi had said, Tommy expected the police to roll up and take him away. He was guilty. Their story, shoddy. But so far, things had remained in a holding pattern.

Tommy had withdrawn, began skipping school. He avoided his sister and Rowan. He knew they blamed him, and truth be told, he blamed himself. The plan had been his idea, the cover story his idea, and each passing day ate at him. He was spiraling into a deep depression.

Rowan sat on the bed next to him. He'd been ignoring her text messages for days and had no desire to speak with her. After everything that happened, he fully expected the gravity of the situation to weigh on her until she caved and sang like a canary. It hadn't happened yet, but there was no doubt in his mind that in time, she would spill the beans.

"Talk to me, Tommy," she said, tears in her eyes.

"There's nothing to say anymore."

"You can't just shut me out. I'm your girlfriend. Please."

She was wrong. He could shut her out, and that was exactly what he intended on doing. And there was that word: *girlfriend*. He wanted nothing to do with dating anymore. There was too much going on in his mind to put forth effort. To be present for another person when he didn't want to be present for himself.

"You know what?" Tommy said, turning to her. "I think we should break up. Then you don't have to worry about me shutting you out. You can worry about yourself. I don't need you. I don't need anyone."

"What? That's not what I meant. I'm worried because I care about you. I don't want to break up."

But Tommy thought that was a lie. He could see it in her eyes. The way she looked at him. She thought he was a murderer. She might be telling him that she didn't want to break up, but how could that be true? One thing was certain: he didn't want a girlfriend. And a relationship is a two-way street. As far as he was concerned, they were as good as finished.

"Just leave me alone. We're through." It hurt his heart to say it, but he knew it was the truth. Maybe if they had been able to rescue Joey, things would be different. But they didn't, and things weren't.

"I'll see you at the funeral, but after that, please, I want space."

Rowan stood up and opened his bedroom door. "You're an asshole, Tommy. I can't believe you."

She slammed the door behind her while Tommy stared at the ceiling.

He had just broken up with his girlfriend and felt nothing.

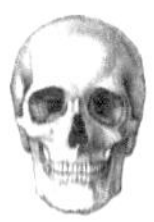

Jackie stood by her bedroom door, listening to everything. She hadn't been trying to snoop, but the walls were thin and sound traveled in their house. She found herself hanging on every word. Tommy had been acting like a prick ever since the accident, rude to both her and Rowan. Rowan deserved better than that, and so did she. He rarely spoke anymore, and truth be told, she didn't want to speak to him. Joey's death had been an accident, but Tommy didn't have to punch him, even if he was standing up for her.

He deserved this, and Jackie would be lying if she said she wasn't eating this shit up right now.

When she heard his bedroom door slam, she opened her own and saw Rowan standing outside his door, crying. Rowan was a bright, beautiful young woman, and didn't deserve to hurt like this. But Tommy? Tommy did deserve to hurt.

"Rowan, are you okay?" she asked.

She didn't answer, just shook her head.

Jackie opened her arms for a hug and embraced her brother's ex-girlfriend.

9

Tommy stood in the cemetery, dressed in all black with the sun beating down overhead. There had been a delay with the services because Mr. Harrison refused to go through with them, not believing that Joey's body could not be recovered. Tommy could understand, though. He imagined the loss of one's son was hard enough to cope with, but to then be told that the body couldn't be recovered from a still body of water? It made no sense.

He pulled at his suit, trying to fan himself with the funeral attire. He was uncomfortable, and not just because of the heat. He had caused this, and now he was here, standing next to his sister and his ex-girlfriend. The two of them seemed to have gotten awful close since he broke up with Rowan, and that only further added to his discomfort.

The entire town had come out to grieve the loss of Joey Harrison. His best friend, dead by his own hand. For the residents of Budlong, the summer had only just begun and yet it was already ruined, the specter of Joey's death looming large.

Graduation had been a few days ago, so there hadn't been enough time for the school to compile any sort of tribute. There wasn't even a dedication in the school's yearbook, given that the project had been completed months ago. They'd done a candlelight vigil. The yearbook dedication would have to wait for the following school year. That is, of course, if everyone hadn't forgotten Joey's death by then. There was always another tragedy, another dead kid. Because that was the world these days. School shootings, mass murders, war, famine, social and political upheaval. There was so much happening on any given day that much of Budlong will likely have forgotten him in a few months, never mind a year from now.

There had been a wake, closed casket, of course. You couldn't view a body that couldn't be found. Tommy could not make heads or tails of it. Sure, the lake was large, but it wasn't like the body could have drifted off to sea. It couldn't have just disappeared and it wasn't like the lake critters could have disposed of the body *that* quickly.

In front of the entire gathering, the pastor droned on, his words bringing some to tears, while others listened in silence. Jackie sobbed uncontrollably, and Tommy only managed to squeeze out a few tears. He worried his lack of waterworks would be proof of his guilt to the small town of Budlong. Aside from the detectives, nobody had come outright and blamed Tommy. But in a place like Budlong, nobody had to. More than likely the detective had been pissed off about getting punked off by Tommy's attorney. Maybe he had leaked that Tommy had been questioned. Either way, word got out and it spread like blight until every person seemed to give him sidelong glances. They didn't have to tell Tommy they blamed him for Joey's death, he *felt* it.

And they were right, he *was* to blame. Everything fell back to him. The prank had been his idea. The punch came from his fist. A part of him tried to pass some of the buck to Jackie, but it wasn't her fault, not really. He knew he never should have told her about what he'd caught Joey doing, never should have convinced her to prank him. She might have been a willing participant, but he had stuffed the cannon and lit the fuse. The knowledge that he was responsible for the death—even if it was accidental—was a burden he would endure the rest of his life. However long that may be. There were times when Tommy didn't feel like pressing on, and wanted to end it all. At night he envisioned taking a toaster bath, or even driving his parents' car off the Newport Bridge. The specifics didn't matter so much, just as long as he could escape the depths of depression that made him feel as if *he* were the one drowning. And in a way, he was. In those dark times, his mind was the worst place to be, yet he could never escape it; he was trapped, a prisoner in his own brain.

The entire thing had been one horrible accident, he hadn't *meant* to kill Joey, but at the end of the day, Joey was dead by his doing, and that was a fact that weighed heavily upon Tommy's soul—a concept he had never believed in but now hoped was such a thing, for then, and only then, would Joey exist in some form.

When the funeral was over, after Mr. Harrison had tossed the first handful of dirt on his only son's casket, and the well-wishers had all moved on, both the Ross twins stayed behind. Mr. Harrison had asked to speak with them when everything was over. Tommy's heart had skipped a beat at the request.

On the one hand, Tommy worried Mr. Harrison had been clued in to what really happened. It was possible. Tommy had never found his phone; its last location on the GPS was Mr. Harrison's boat, and he didn't have the balls to ask the man if he could search the boat where he'd killed his son. Rather than go looking for it, he'd simply had his parents get him a new one. It took a bit of convincing; his folks were smart enough to know that the locator should lead them to the phone, but when it came down to it, Tommy had leaned into the tragedy and tugged at their heartstrings, knowing they'd acquiesce, wanting to tiptoe around their son rather than argue with him.

On the other hand, it was entirely possible Mr. Harrison had no clue and simply wanted to speak with the twins. Tommy had been Joey's best friend, after all. Maybe he wanted one last chat before everyone inevitably moved on.

Tommy saw the odds as a coin flip, and when Mr. Harrison approached to speak about whatever was on his mind, Tommy began to sweat even more, if that were somehow possible. His nerves were on edge as Mr. Harrison approached, but quickly put at ease when the man ignored his extended hand, instead opting to pull him in for a hug.

"Tommy, how are you holding up?" Mr. Harrison nodded at Jackie. "And you, too, Jackie, how are you doing?"

"Us? We should be asking you that, sir. I can't imagine your loss, we are so, so sorry," Tommy said. Jackie sobbed, her lips quivered, unable to summon even the briefest of condolences.

"It's tough, I won't lie. Eighteen is far too young for a life to be snuffed out. A father should never outlive their child. And those damn pigs can't seem to find his remains. Jackie, I owe you an apology. If my son did that to you, please, forgive him. I've never known him to be a predator. Clearly the boy wasn't capable of handling his alcohol, but that's no excuse for what he did to you." Tears welled in his eyes.

Tommy bit his lower lip and looked anywhere *but* Mr. Harrison's eyes. To look him in the eye might betray the truth. Tommy was a coward, he knew it. But he couldn't help it. The shame was too much. To make things more awkward, not only was he lying to the man, he was trying to console him. What right did he have? The cops hadn't believed the web of lies they spun, but Mr. Harrison seemed to have taken it hook, line, and sinker. He felt lower than low. Just standing here in his presence was enough to make him squirm. "Listen, Mr. Harrison, I just want to say—"

Mr. Harrison cut him off. There was a brief flash of *something* in his eyes. Anger? But as quickly as it appeared it was gone, replaced with the hurt once more. "Tommy, please. No need to apologize or explain every-thing. I understand. Accidents happen, right? It's not like there's some sort of conspiracy"—he looked at Jackie—"and again, I'm sorry for my son's behavior. I don't know what would possess him to do such a thing, and I can't stop feeling like it was my fault. If I had just taken the keys to the boat with me, he wouldn't have accosted you the way he did. It isn't you guys who should be shouldering the blame. I was wrong to place so much trust in the boy. If not for my misplaced trust, Joey would be alive today and none of us would be standing here now, would we?"

Something about the way Mr. Harrison spoke bothered Tommy, wriggled its way into his brain like a worm burrowing into his ear. The tone of his voice, odd. Inflection, off. And the way he mentioned the accident and using words like conspiracy . . . Why would he even say something like that? He couldn't know, could he? It had to be Tommy's guilt and anxiety, there was no way he knew.

"Mr. Harrison, you aren't to blame, truly. If you can stand here and forgive me for my part in the fight that led to this, and tell me it isn't my fault, regardless of the reason *why* we fought, then I can tell you it isn't your fault either. Sometimes shit happens, ya know?"

"Yeah, you're right about that, Tommy. Shit does happen, doesn't it?"

An awkward silence replaced the odd conversation. But Tommy preferred the silence over walking on eggshells. Eventually, Mr. Harrison broke the uncomfortable silence. "Speaking of shit happening," he started, "I know Joey was going to have a graduation-slash-end of summer-slash-going off to college party at one of our lake cabins. If you guys wanted to still do that, maybe celebrate Joey's life one last time, I would be more than happy to let you use one of the cabins in honor of my son."

Tommy was shocked. The man couldn't be serious, could he?

"No, we couldn't. I wouldn't feel right," Tommy said.

"I insist. Joey was really looking forward to it, and I know it's what he would want. Give me a month or so to clean the place up, then I'll let you guys have your crack at the place before I open it up to Airbnb renters."

"Seriously? Man, Mr. Harrison, that would be so cool, but, like, you're *sure* you don't mind? You aren't just saying something you don't mean?"

"Tommy, one thing I want you to know about me is that everything I say and do is not without meaning. I told you I want you guys to have the party. I mean it. Just let me know when you're gonna do it. I won't accept no for an answer." Mr. Harrison hesitated for a bit and said, "You owe it to Joey," and then, "We all do."

Mr. Harrison left after the odd exchange, leaving Tommy feeling utterly confused about the conversation that had just transpired.

"That was weird, right, Jackie? It's not just me? Please tell me he was behaving oddly," Tommy said.

At last, able to get words to formulate, her chin still quivering but no longer crying, Jackie finally spoke, "Of course he was behaving oddly. His son is dead. It would be weird if he *wasn't* behaving strangely."

What could Tommy say to that? It was true, he knew what they'd done.

Quiet as the graves they stood amongst, the Ross twins left the cemetery.

Tommy was already thinking of how much he didn't want to throw a party at the lake. Part of it was the depression he'd been suffering ever since the incident, but it was more than that. It was such an odd request. Joey was dead, and now that the funeral was behind them, Tommy wanted nothing more than to allow the memory of his one-time best friend to die too.

10

J ackie gave herself a final once-over in the mirror. Everything needed to be on point.

Hair. Check.

Makeup. Check.

Outfit. Check.

She applied the same standards to her bedroom, which she now thought of as a set, and lighting too. The ring light and phone were ready to go, the set was clean. Nothing out of place, nothing in view of the camera that shouldn't be.

Jackie put a lot of time and effort into her social media presence. Truth be told, she always had. All the boys at school had always followed her, and disgustingly enough, older men too. At first, she only posted pictures of herself. She was a pretty girl and proud of it. If boys, or man-boys, couldn't control themselves, that wasn't her problem. Regardless, her platform had grown over the years, especially since she'd turned eighteen, just before everything had happened with Joey. Practically overnight, her following had skyrocketed, as if all these men were waiting for the moment she turned eighteen to hit that *Follow* button. The more she thought about it, the more she realized that was probably precisely what happened.

Not long after the accident that resulted in Joey's death, Jackie had really contemplated life and the direction she wanted hers to go in. She wasn't 100 percent sure what she wanted to be. She had always wanted to be a nurse, but lately, after Joey had died, she was stuck in a rut and no longer had the drive to pursue a nursing degree. That night had changed her, and she no longer felt the same desire she once did to rush off to school. She had no plans for the distant future. But what she *did* know was that her future no longer included college. Jackie sure as hell wasn't about to go hundreds of thousands of dollars in debt for a loan that, if she was lucky, would help land her a job making $100,000 a year or less. Especially not in today's economy, where, in the state of Rhode Island, if you were "middle class," you couldn't afford to live anymore. Anything less than $200,000 a year and you had no hope of living a comfortable life. Her parents were always talking about inflation, and the rising price of literally every single good or commodity, and to her, the math didn't add up.

The ball really got rolling when one weekend some skeezeball old man messaged her on Instagram. He was looking for a sugar baby and thought she might be a good fit. And while the prospect of getting paid a ton of money tax-free sounded great to her, the idea of some wrinkly geezer lying on top of her and pumping away sounded far less appealing. It was repulsive. She had choked back vomit and then blocked the pervert.

But the interaction had also planted a seed, and when

she was scrolling through various social media platforms the seed sprouted into a full-blown idea. She didn't need to be a sugar baby to take the money off horny men. And she certainly didn't need to sleep with anyone to do it. Women, not much older than her, were becoming rich from platforms like OnlyFans, using their social media accounts to funnel people to the website hosting their "content." Why couldn't she do the same? She could show as little or as much as she wanted, in the comfort of her own home, and make a ton of money while she figured out exactly what she wanted to do with her post-high school life. And truth be told, it was the first time anything had excited her since before the accident. It quickly became a way for her to keep her mind off what they'd done, an escape from the horrible reality that had become her life.

Well, maybe not the first time. She had recently begun seeing someone. It started off innocent enough. That night she saw Rowan crying in the hallway, she'd only intended on comforting her, and if she was being honest, becoming better friends with her so Tommy would have to deal with his ex being around all the time.

But things escalated quickly, and not only did they grow thick as thieves, but Jackie began to have feelings for her. Falling for another woman wasn't what had surprised her. She'd always been attracted to both men and women, and she believed people should be free to be with whoever they wanted. It was nobody's business but their own. However, the fact that she'd fallen for Rowan of all people, *that* was the surprise. It wasn't that she was in love with her. In her young life she'd had infatuations, strong feelings for people, but she always thought *true love* was a feeling that you would *know* when it happened. There would be no questions about it. She didn't feel that way about Rowan, but she did like her. A lot.

Jackie forced the thoughts out of her head. She couldn't think about Rowan right now; it was a distraction and she needed to focus on creating videos and photos. That was another thing that impressed Jackie about Rowan, she didn't seem to care about what Jackie was doing alone. She didn't like it, but she understood it was strictly business, and that it was helping her get through tough times. So while she might not be happy about it, she supported Jackie's unorthodox approach to financial security. These days, people were much more accepting of what Jackie was doing than they would have been even five years ago. And thankfully, Rowan was one of the accepting ones.

Clicking the remote that controlled her phone, she started the video, going through a small dance routine that accentuated her curves and left them jiggling, the exact type of thing most likely to draw some horny, incel prick to her paid content.

Halfway through her second routine, the lights in the house cut off.

Dammit!

Jackie waited for the lights to kick back on but they never did. It struck her as odd, the lights staying off, because by that point, the generator should have picked up the slack.

A few years back they had a major snowstorm on Christmas Eve, a nor'easter that left much of the state without power for days. They'd gotten by okay, but the neighboring town of Glenwood had suffered a string of grisly murders during the outage. A recently released inmate had committed several murders throughout the town, including murdering an entire family in their home. And Glenwood Memorial Hospital had been the scene of a second, grislier rampage. Ever since then, her father swore they'd never be without power again.

"I guess I've gotta do everything myself," she muttered as she removed her phone from the ring light and toggled the flashlight on the device. She aimed the light in front of her and exited the room, slowly making her way toward the basement. As she approached the top of the steps, her skin broke out in goose bumps. Someone stepped over her grave, her mother would say. She shivered involuntarily. Jackie wasn't afraid of the dark, but sometimes you couldn't help what direction your mind ran off in. It was unusual for both the power and the generator to fail. She'd like to think it was a special circumstance and chose to show herself grace. Besides, nobody was home to judge her.

At the bottom of the stairs, she turned the corner, moving quickly through the dark. The flashlight did a great job keeping the darkness at bay, but even if that weren't the case, they'd lived in the house as far back as Jackie could remember, so she didn't need the light to get around. It was a security blanket more than anything.

Across from the door to the basement, Jackie noticed the home's rear entry door ajar. The breeze rushing in was warm but did nothing to alleviate the chill running through her body.

Did someone break in? Should I run out the front door?

Jackie unlocked the screen and texted her dad to let him know the power was out, then opened the call app on the phone and input 911, but stopped short of hitting the dial button. She would hold off on calling, not wanting to suffer the embarrassment of an emergency call for an empty house, but she figured having the number ready to dial might be a smart idea. Skeptical as she was, Jackie had seen enough horror movies to know what came next.

But she still made her way to the basement, closing the rear entry door as she walked by it. Taking the steps two at a time, Jackie reached the bottom in what might have been a world record. At this point, she wasn't worried about alerting someone to her presence, she just wanted to get the lights on ASAP.

At least the basement didn't look like the setting of a *Saw* movie. It was immaculately finished, and more comfortable even than the main living area upstairs. The space was dry, bright, and well furnished. Jackie made her way to the other side of the basement and opened the circuit box. The main breaker had been flicked off. That was odd, she didn't know what could have tripped it. She was no electrician, and flipping switches was the extent of her knowledge of breakers, diagnosing them wasn't part of her skill set.

Her phone pinged. It was her father. She opened the notification.

Check the breakers. See if any switches are flipped off. If anything is off, flip it on, problem solved. If you get the power back on, can you please check the generator? I thought it had gas, but maybe it's out. I'll get more on the way home if it's empty.

"Yeah, great, Dad. I already fixed it," she said as she tapped away at her phone.

Ok, Dad. Got the power back on, it was the main

switch. I'll check the generator in a minute and let you know.

Jackie headed back up the basement stairs, exited the house, and made her way to the generator. She looked around until she found the fuel gauge; the arrow pointed to full. Out of the corner of her eye, she noticed frayed wires on the side of the generator. The motion lights flicked off so she took a few steps closer, tripping the sensor and illuminating the yard.

She looked at the wires, clearly tampered with, but that wasn't what stopped her in her tracks. Her dog, Bully, lay next to the wires, his body still. Her initial thought, before she'd gotten closer for a better look, was that Bully had electrocuted himself by chewing the wires. But that was definitely not the case. The dog's underside was ripped wide open, its internal organs pulled from within and left in a heaping pile behind the dog's back. Bully's head was also cocked at an unusual angle, his neck broken. A puddle of blood was spreading beneath the English Bulldog.

This had been done recently.

Jackie screamed and fumbled her phone, but caught it before it hit the ground. She tapped the screen, sending the call to 911. The moment she put the phone to her ear she heard a grunt and felt a heavy impact against the back of her head.

Her world turned black. She was unconscious before her body hit the ground.

11

The moment the baseball bat cracked the little bitch in the head, the driveway lit up like a Christmas tree and he could hear tires crunching over gravel. He turned around and beat feet as fast as possible, dropping the aluminum Louisville Slugger right next to the girl's body. He'd almost turned around to try to snatch it and get the hell out of Dodge before getting caught, but thought better of it. Luckily, he'd worn gloves; at least he hadn't fucked that up. This was a lesson. He was doing things different, acting impulsively rather than sticking to the tried and true methods he'd honed over time. As a result, he'd come shockingly close to being discovered. Leaving the girl meant a loose end. He hated loose ends.

Sprinting through the neighborhood yards, hopping fences, and squeezing through bushes, he eventually emerged a few blocks down the road where he had parked his car. He popped the trunk, pulled his ski mask off, and removed the gloves from his hands, tossing them all in a Ziploc bag stored in the spare tire compartment.

Police sirens cut through the quiet night, but he paid them no mind. He took his time getting into the driver's seat, then finding a music playlist to listen to on the drive home. He'd intentionally parked the car far enough away that nobody would place him at the scene of the crime, even if he were to be stopped and questioned. And he knew that as long as he looked like he belonged, the likelihood of being stopped was slim. It would be a shame if the thing that led to his capture was something as routine as a speeding ticket.

He started the car and drove off. The night was sure to be a long one. The little bitch was safe, but he still had another one to play with. He'd toyed with her since the night he found her on the side of the road—a gift placed right in his lap. But now it was time to end that one and give his full attention to bigger and better things.

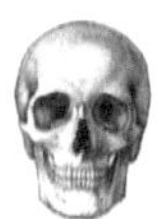

The man walked into the room, and though her situation had changed, something seemed different this time. The sarcastic, witty comments that usually preceded the torture were absent, replaced by a haunting silence, which to her was far scarier. Her gut told her this was the end, and that was fine by her. She wanted the torture to end, needed it to end. With each cut, each broken bone, each amputation, a piece of her had died, and she finally lost the will to live. Her tormentor, however, had not lost his desire for a plaything. Until now.

When he grew tired of staring at her in silence, he said, "It's time. I had my fun and you were a wonderful guest, but something that requires my undivided attention has come up."

He walked away for a moment. Lucy couldn't see what he was doing, but she could hear the clanging of metal, the rustling of plastic. Were they bags? Was it a tarp? She didn't know, didn't care. He'd confirmed what she already knew. A tear slid down her cheek. Not from fear, not from sadness, but from the sheer joy of knowing that she would no longer be subjected to the unfathomable pain she'd been put through. She had no idea how long she'd been there, had no concept of time. The room had no windows so it was impossible to know the rising and setting of the sun. Even if she had been keeping track somehow, the amount of times she'd lost consciousness would have made it impossible anyway. She breathed a sigh of relief.

Then she heard the sound of a chain saw starting and revving up. She screamed, struggled underneath the restraints holding her to the table.

She thought she was ready to accept death, but not like this—to be slaughtered like an animal.

Footsteps approached and the loud motor drowned out the sound of her screaming, even in her own head.

When the power tool hit her neck she felt a searing pain, blood splattered, and then she felt nothing more.

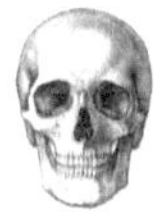

He felt better already. He hated to rush time with his playthings, but finishing this one would allow him to tend to more pressing matters.

Like the fuckers who'd killed his son. While he was

depositing Lucy's severed remains into the heavy-duty trash bags he'd brought with him, the thought of what he would do to the teens brought a smile to his face. Was it because he knew he'd kill again so soon? Or because he knew justice would be had? He didn't know, and frankly, he didn't care. Feelings weren't something he dealt with often, and he didn't know how to navigate them. Hell, most of his life he'd never really felt anything for Joey. But it was personal, even if he didn't really love his son the way a father should. Couldn't love his son in the traditional way. There was a disconnect in his brain which wouldn't allow trivial things such as love to cloud his mind.

But despite not truly loving his son, it didn't change the fact that Joey was *his*, and he didn't like when people messed with his things.

Still, he knew he must proceed with caution. Years of meticulous planning, watching over his shoulder, and distancing himself from his kills allowed him to do what he did best without getting caught. But in his desire for revenge, he'd slipped and almost brought it all crashing down. He wanted an early taste of what he was going to do to three of them, and he wanted to pay special attention to the whore who'd coerced his son. Who portrayed him as a sex offender to the authorities. He'd almost paid for his mistake.

Almost.

But he was still a free man. And so the whore, along with her brother and their friend would be the ones paying soon enough. He simply needed to stay the course. Once he had his revenge, maybe he'd be caught. But at that point, it would no longer matter. He would have had a good run, and if he was brought to justice for what he did to them, so be it. He had been getting away with murder for years, knew it was unlikely he'd be able to do so forever. All good things come to an end, and he'd been an active serial killer for almost two decades. He thought about his deeds, past and future and he found himself coming to terms with the inevitable end of it. It didn't matter. He'd found that in life, nothing ever did.

As he rolled up the tarps he'd laid out, something he saw on a television show, he found himself pondering the finale. There would be a lot of the graduates there, why limit himself to just his son's murderers? Why not get as many of them as he could? Really go out with a bang.

When he finished with the cleanup—Lucy's DNA scrubbed from existence, her remains wrapped in tarps and trash bags—he looked around his kill room and felt nothing. There was a time when basking it in gave him a great sense of pride. Of Accomplishment. Now, the only excitement he felt was for what was to come. He'd given the teens permission to use the property: given them the keys and told them that was confirmation enough, they had his permission to use the premises, though he wouldn't be around. He'd be away on a business trip. Of course there was no business trip, but they wouldn't need to know that. With them not expecting him, it meant they'd let loose more. The booze would flow and they would let their guards down. The only thing on their minds: hoping the cops wouldn't break up their little party. They'd be at ease. Ripe for the kill.

He smiled at the thought.

Mr. Harrison walked to the wall switch and was about to cut the lights when he felt his foot squish something. He looked down at a dark substance. Thick, viscous. At first, he thought he'd somehow botched the cleanup. It was possible, especially with how careless he'd been recently, but those thoughts were quickly dashed. The stuff on the floor was most definitely *not* blood. Any questions about that were answered when it began traveling up his foot.

"What the fuck!" he said, jumping back. His foot stuck for a moment before freeing itself with a loud puckering noise. With a gloved hand he peeled the black shit off his leg. There was a hole in his pants where the thing had been, and his leg burned. He flicked it onto the floor and his glove sizzled. The thing landed with a *splat* before zipping back to the much larger puddle which had crept from beneath the door and began somehow rising, taking a more solid shape.

Mr. Harrison was a psychopath, he knew that, but had he finally lost his mind too? The ooze was growing, bubbling, rising to almost three feet in height now, like something out of one of his son's movies. But this was no movie. This was real life, live in the flesh, and he was watching as the tar-colored substance rose to full human height, looking very much the shape of a human. Arms, legs, a head with hairlike texture carved out, falling down to shoulder length.

He was panicking now. Sweating bullets. His heart pounded in his chest as he scrambled to figure out what to do. There was only one exit, and that was blocked by this abomination. And though it was the shape of a human woman, the face was featureless, which made it all the more terrifying. Mr. Harrison looked around, his mind running in circles trying to figure out how to get himself out of this situation. His eyes fell upon the chain saw in the corner of the room. "Aha!" he said in triumph. He'd cut his way out. Plenty of people had met their end at the mercy of his chain saw; this fucking thing would meet the same fate. Everything ends eventually, and so, too, would this . . . whatever the fuck it was.

He ran to the chain saw and his heart skipped a beat when it wouldn't start. The thing stalked forward, tendrils whipping off its body, snapping at the air like Indiana Jones's whip. He tried a few more times but no dice, the fucking thing wouldn't start. He felt like he was going to puke. This was it. He was hyperventilating now and though he always figured when death came he would welcome it with open arms, now it was knocking on his doorstep and he was ready to cry. He was going to go out like a bitch.

Closer now, the thing let out a moan, as if it were trying to speak, but no words came out. Its shape was changing again, growing taller, broader. A male humanoid form. The texture of the hair changed, no longer a wavy feminine style, it started to look more like a crew cut. The body became more detailed, as if it were learning to mimic the human form better. First, chest muscles formed, and then the face became more defined, had features somehow, yet they were . . . off. A copycat attempting to replicate the normalcy of the human form, yet failing to do so. Still, Mr. Harrison recognized the face and looked on in wide-eyed horror as a thought crossed his mind. *It's Joey.* But how? How the fuck could that be? To anyone else, they might not notice it, but Mr. Harrison knew his son when he saw him.

"Daaaa," the thing croaked in a guttural, alien tone.

"Jo-Joey," he stuttered, frozen in place.

In the blink of an eye, two lumps formed on his son's

chest, growing to a point before ejecting with incredible force, each one hitting Mr. Harrison in opposing shoulders, driving him into the wall behind him, pinning him in place.

He screamed, the pain was immense, only exceeded by his newfound fear of mortality.

The Joey-thing moved forward, blobs of ooze dripping onto the floor, splattering, and re-bonding with the larger form. Its face shifted back to the female form before losing that and eventually becoming a featureless blob with two empty eye sockets and a line where the mouth should be. It stopped next to the discarded chain saw and a tendril shot out, snatching the tool and pulling it toward the thing's mass, where it was enveloped in the black substance.

It moaned and Mr. Harrison was thankful it didn't call him Dad again. The feeling of gratitude was quickly dashed when the thing raised a bubbling arm with stringy sections of the mass writhing over themselves, growing larger, shifting. In the blink of an eye, the arm was gone, replaced by an organic, pitch-black chain saw

"What the fuck!" Mr. Harrison screamed. "Please, no. God, no." But God, real or not, would not save him. Not after the things he'd done. He'd resorted to the same base instinct everyone did at the end of their lives, pleading to a higher power they never believed in.

The chain saw revved, and the sound was horrific. The machine-like noise was replaced with an eerie squealing. Whatever this thing was, it seemed to be attempting to mimic even the sound of the power tool it had absorbed.

The thing plodded forward, dripping onto the floor and reabsorbing the material with each step.

Plop. Plop. Plop.

The chain saw thrusted forward. Mr. Harrison struggled to move out of the way but it was no use, he was impaled through the shoulders and pinned to the wall; he couldn't budge an inch.

Skin tore. Flesh and blood sprayed, splattering the thing, the walls, the ceiling, the floor. The human flesh that splattered against the creature was immediately taken on as part of the whole. The saw continued to rip and tear through flesh, muscle, and bone until there was nothing but splattered blood and chunks of meat stuck to various surfaces.

The monster's form once again shifted. At first, transforming to a grotesque approximation of Mr. Harrison before finally resorting to the formless ooze it had been, this time much larger than before. Black tendrils shot out, grabbing the chunks of meat and pulling them into its body even as smaller bits of the ooze detached itself, sliding across the floor, walls, and ceiling in a sluglike movement, sucking up the remnants of the man's body. When no trace of Mr. Harrison was to be found, the monstrosity made quick work of the trash bags containing the remains of Lucy, as if it had sensed the pieces of her within. The thing bubbled, grew larger, and then eventually flattened, shrinking in size but growing wider in length before sliding underneath the door and disappearing to wherever it had come from.

12

———

Tommy sat on a cheap, plastic reclining chair in the hospital room where his sister lay on the bed, conscious, but still clearly feeling the effects of the blow to the head she'd taken. It had been a good one too. The doctor had told their parents that by sheer luck, it appeared Jackie had sustained no serious injuries, though they wanted her to remain at the hospital overnight for observation. Mom and Dad had agreed, of course. They were worried sick. Mom especially. Dad had taken her for a walk; she couldn't stand the sight of her only daughter laid up in the hospital.

It had been their father who'd discovered Jackie's unconscious body, lying in a pool of blood, a mixture of both hers and the family dog's. What kind of sick fuck would do something like that? The responding officer had told Dad the assault must have taken place just before he'd arrived home. Showing up when he did had more than likely spooked the perpetrator, saving his daughter's life. They'd asked all sorts of questions, and sometimes it felt like those questions were insinuating Dad was a suspect. Other questions seemed to imply Jackie's assailant may have been someone close to the family, or possibly a deranged fan.

That particular thread had really sent their parents into a spiral, because up until that moment, they hadn't known about Jackie's OnlyFans account. It had been Tommy who'd told the detective about it. He'd done it for two reasons. Number one, it was the only thing that made sense. Obviously Dad hadn't done it; he wasn't even home at the time. Who else would creep around their house, maim their dog, and attack his sister? An internet weirdo, that's who.

The other reason he'd done it had been pure spite. Yes, he loved his sister, and was deeply concerned for her safety and well-being, but he was still pissed-off and disgusted that Jackie was now messing around with his ex-girlfriend. That was just fucked-up. It was like Bro Code, but for siblings. You don't date your sibling's ex. The relationship between Tommy and Jackie had been rocky after the prank and Joey's death, but Jackie and Rowan hooking up had obliterated what was left of it. So yeah, he *did* still care for his sister. But that didn't mean he wasn't going to petty when the opportunity arose.

He heard Jackie stirring on the bed, watched her try to sit up. "Don't move," he said, "just lie back and relax."

She winced in pain but laughed. "Relax? Someone tried to fucking kill me. How am I supposed to relax?"

She had a point and he felt stupid for saying it, but it had just come out. One of those things you say because you don't know what else to say and it was the only thing that seemed right in the moment. "Good point."

"Tommy, you're a piece of shit—"

He shook his head. "Listen, you had it com—"

"Let me finish. You're a piece of shit, but you're my brother, and I love you. Please, I don't want to keep being at odds like this."

"So you're going to stop fucking with my ex?"

"No. I don't know. I need time to think. I did it to piss you off at first, but I really like her. This is bigger than that. I almost died. What if something worse happened to me, and we never got a chance to fix what's going on between us?"

Another good point. Lovers come and go, especially at their age. Was he really willing to write off his sister for good over Rowan? In the grand scheme of things, he knew it was nothing. But that didn't take the sting off. They were young adults, still teenagers. Everything seemed so big, so important. But at the end of the day, when Rowan was gone from both of their lives, they'd still have each other. Unless he let something as stupid as a lover tear them apart.

"I don't want to keep fighting, either," he said. "But I'm pissed-off. How would you feel if I was banging your boyfriend behind your back?"

"She's not your girlfriend anymore, Tommy. She hasn't been for a while."

"That's not the damn point, Jackie!"

"I know it's not. For what it's worth, I'm sorry."

Tears welled up in his eyes. There had been too much hurt lately, but she was right. Losing his sister would only add to the pain, not make things better.

"I'm sorry, too," he said.

And he meant it. It would take time for what she did

to him to stop hurting. To build up trust again. And he wasn't sure he *would* be able to trust her around future girlfriends. But blood was thicker than water, and he loved his sister. Seeing her here in the hospital, knowing how much worse it could have been, *almost had been*, was all the push he needed to try to move on and bury the hatchet.

Tommy stood up and moved to her bedside. He grabbed her hand, careful not to mess with any of the medical equipment connected to her. She squeezed his hand. He squeezed back, gently. "Okay, Jackie, we're good."

"I love you, even if you're a prick," she said. Despite the situation, they shared a laugh.

"You think Mom and Dad are still gonna let us have the party? she asked.

He looked at her, puzzled. "You still wanna go through with it?"

"Yeah, I do. If anything, I want to do it even more. Who knows when something could happen to either one of us? Joey is gone and I got lucky. I don't want to worry that I could be gone any minute and live my life afraid to do fun things."

"Well, when you put it that way, I guess you're right. Mom and Dad? I don't know what they're gonna say. Between this, and Dad finding out about what you're doing online, he's definitely gonna go off on you. *But,* we're eighteen. We're adults. He really can't do anything to stop us."

"He could kick us out."

"Mom wouldn't let him. And anyway, even if she would allow it, after what happened tonight, I think he'd rather have us as close by as possible. Even if he is furious with us."

"So we're really gonna do this? I mean, it doesn't feel sleazy to you, throwing a graduation party, after we've already graduated, in honor of Joey . . . after what we did to him?"

Tommy's face went slack. "Yeah, it kinda does. But it wasn't our idea. Mr. Harrison has a point. Joey *would* have wanted one last party before everyone went their separate ways. He'd feel differently if he knew we were involved, but he doesn't, and we already agreed we would continue to live as if it were just an accident. And yeah, our fight *did* cause him to drown, but at the same time, it *was* just an accident. I didn't mean for him to die," Tommy said.

He could tell by the look in his sister's eyes that she didn't believe him. But it was the truth. Of course he hadn't meant for this to happen. People fight all the time, but it was just a freak accident.

Just because they agreed to carry out their lives insisting that it was a freak accident didn't mean the knowledge of the truth was suddenly washed away. He shouldered the grief, the pain, every single day, and probably would until the day he died. Hollow words didn't absolve you of your sins. He knew that now. Surely Jackie did too. But what else could they do? He wasn't about to admit guilt and toss his own life away. There was still no doubt in his mind they would at least attempt a manslaughter charge on him, and certainly if Mr. Harrison knew the truth he would push for it, had the money and the connections to do so. No, better to carry the burden in secret than throw away another life.

There was a knock on the door before it gradually

opened. Tommy and Jackie both looked up, expecting their parents to return. Rowan stepped into the room, the look on her face one of both horror and relief that her girlfriend, though brutally attacked, was relatively okay.

Tommy's stomach turned sour, a pit forming in his gut. "All right, I'll come back later," he said.

"Tommy, wait, I thought—"

"I'm fine. I just need to go for a walk, that's all."

He made his way across the room, nodded at Rowan, giving her a cold greeting. He may have buried that hatchet with his sister, but that didn't mean he wasn't still upset with Rowan. In time maybe he could forgive her, probably would, but for now he wanted nothing more than to escape her presence.

He closed the door behind him, cutting off their hushed whispers. And though he was relieved to be away from Rowan, he felt more alone than ever before. Maybe the party would be good for him, one last hurrah signaling the end of this stage of his life and the beginning of a future where he could put the past behind him, leave the guilt and shame buried at the bottom of Lake Budlong where it belonged.

13

The days passed uneventfully, preparations to the cabin where they'd throw the party were coming along slowly but surely. Everything was almost complete. Tommy felt much better knowing as soon as it was over he'd be out of this damned town starting his life fresh. Earlier in the year, he was convinced he had the world at his fingertips. He had been excited to get off to college, but ever since the accident, he'd become less sure. Now, he was no longer excited, and it was a toss-up between college or going straight into the workforce. Truth be told, neither of those options seemed appealing to him. To cover his bases, he had registered at one of the out-of-town campuses of the state's community college, though if he did end up going to school, he would probably skip the fall semester and start in the spring with a clear mind. He needed a break. Needed time to think things through.

That had been another argument with his father, who'd told him if he wasn't going to jump right into school he was welcome to take his ass elsewhere.

Fine by Tommy, he hadn't planned on staying in this godforsaken place anyway. There was too much pain here. Memories, ghosts.

Rowan had sent out an email blast to the entire graduating class and it seemed like there would be a big turnout. Some of the jocks had volunteered to bring copious amounts of alcohol—one of the perks of having a sister most of your peers pined for. Another member of their class, whose family owned the local pizza joint, had convinced her parents to donate more pizza than they could hope to eat, even if three-quarters of the class showed up.

Tommy, Rowan, and Jackie had all put in equal amounts of elbow grease cleaning up the cabin. They were thankful to Mr. Harrison for letting them use the place, but it would have been nice if he'd lent them a property that hadn't been abandoned for so long. Repairs and maintenance had been kept up, but it was clear from the amount of dust and debris inside that the premises had been long vacant and Mr. Harrison hadn't bothered keeping it clean. At least the busywork had kept Tommy's mind clear, allowing him to focus his thoughts on anything besides his dead best friend.

The three of them sat by the shore of the lake, feet in the water. Tommy was still uncomfortable with the new dynamic but he decided to let it go, or at least try to. Life was too short, a lesson he'd recently learned. A lesson people his age didn't typically learn, although the manner in which he'd stumbled upon the newfound clarity was not something he'd wish on his worst enemy. It was all too much to bear. The pain of losing his best friend, the blame lying squarely on his shoulders, and almost losing his sister shortly after. He'd even lost his high school sweet-heart over it. He'd probably never be as close to Jackie as he once was, and certainly not with Rowan, but maybe they could salvage some of what they once had before they all went their separate ways.

Briefly, Tommy had been excited about the send-off, but now that it was the eve before the party, preparations finished at last, he no longer felt that way. He was at the precipice of a new mountain, the other side of which led to him starting his life over, and *that* was where his focus now lay. Life was funny like that. Six months ago, his past self would have laughed if someone told him he was about to throw the biggest party the town of Budlong had ever seen, and he wanted nothing more than to be done with it.

But that was exactly how he felt.

The warm breeze over the lake ruffled his hair as he stared at the calm water, feeling not only alone in his thoughts, but alone in life as his sister and ex-girlfriend sat a few feet away shoulder to shoulder, whispering about God knows what. He wanted to be happy for them, truly, but he just couldn't bring himself to do it and even though he'd decided to bury the hatchet, their distance from each other while they were hanging out showed how truly apart they really were. And no matter how much they told each other they wanted things to be the same again, it was likely time would drift them further apart, much like a canoe left untied on the lake, drifting from the dock with nobody to pull it to shore.

The two young women stood up and approached him. When his sister spoke, he jumped, completely unaware they'd walked over to him.

"Jesus, don't sneak up on me like that," he said.

"Jumpy much? Nobody snuck up on you, we were sitting right next to you, weirdo," Jackie said.

Rowan elbowed Jackie, a light touch that couldn't have possibly hurt, but Jackie played it up, rubbing her elbow. God, these two really made him sick to his stomach sometimes. They were like a cheesy romance movie cranked up to eleven.

"Fine, I'll be nice. I'm sorry for scaring you, weirdo," Jackie said with an edge of sarcasm in her voice.

"You didn't scare me. I was just thinking, that's all," Tommy said. "It takes a lot more than an e-girl to scare me," Tommy returned the sarcasm right back, knowing his sister wouldn't mind. They still busted each other's balls all the time, regardless of their recently tumultuous relationship. Some things never changed, especially not the barbs exchanged between siblings. But what if things did change when he left town? They'd always be blood, they'd always have the times they shared, but when you cut right down to it, no matter how much they tried to leave the past behind them, the past would always be there. Things were tough for them now. Would time and distance allow for healing, or would it further drive a wedge through their relationship?

Jackie flashed a smile, taking the barb in stride. "You ready for tomorrow?" she asked.

"Yeah, everything's set up and ready to go. The house is clean, the beer and liquor is ready, all we really have to do is pick up the food. Everything came together pretty damn good, if you ask me."

Jackie shook her head. "That's not what I mean."

Of course it wasn't. He knew that. But he didn't want to talk about what she really meant. Because he wasn't ready. He'd killed his best friend and now they were throwing an end of summer graduation party in his honor. How the fuck was he supposed to be ready for something like that? He didn't even want to be there, and would much rather stay home and let the rest of the graduating class do what they will. Who gives a shit about throwing a legendary rager for a bunch of people he didn't give a rat's ass about? Certainly not him, and he didn't think Jackie or Rowan gave a flying fuck either. So why were they even doing this? Because Mr. Harrison had asked them to. The idea was so absurd, but how could they say no with the guilt the three of them harbored?

"I know what you meant. I don't want to talk about it. I want to forget about all of this, but I can't do that until we throw this fucking party. When that's out of the way, I'll feel much better."

"We feel the same way," Rowan said, putting her hand on his shoulder, giving it a gentle squeeze.

Tommy felt repulsed by her touch and flinched, but didn't pull away. He didn't know if she noticed his aversion to her touch; he hoped she did.

"I know you guys do, so let's just get this shit over with and move on. I don't want to live through this anymore," Tommy said as he popped the top on one of the beers they'd brought with them. He tilted the can up and chugged it all in one go while the others watched him. The look plastered on their faces as they witnessed the beer disappear in an instant was one of shock. But Tommy knew they weren't impressed. The look of shock was likely because the effortless way in which he downed it probably had them considering an intervention on his behalf. They weren't wrong. He'd always drank socially at parties, and with Joey, but ever since that night on the lake, and especially after Jackie was assaulted, the social drinking had given way to something much more frequent. He was surprised his parents hadn't noticed because they were the ones he was stealing the alcohol from all summer long. Maybe they were just showing him grace.

Once he polished off the last of the beer, he tossed the empty back in the cooler, grabbed the handle, and made his way along the trail in the direction of the cabin, leaving Jackie and Rowan to follow. He heard their hushed whispers and knew they were talking about him. Oh well, let them talk.

He'd be gone before they knew it. And sooner, rather than later, his drinking problem wouldn't be something they'd have to worry about

14

As the sun set the following evening, the graduating class of Budlong High showed up to the cabin on Lake Budlong in droves. There were a great many in attendance, the long driveway filled to capacity and the narrow road leading to the property was lined with vehicles on both sides. So far, there hadn't been any accidents. No fender benders or side panel scrapings, but as the night wore on and the teens had their fill of alcohol, that was sure to change. There were no neighboring homes to complain about the crowd or the noise as the homes *not* owned by Mr. Harrison's company were located on the other side of the lake. The summer folk would neither see nor hear anything. At least, not until the drunk teens started making their way to the shore to carry on the party by the water. The summer home owners wouldn't care anyway, they were used to lakeside partying, and most of them threw a party or two of their own during the warm season.

Tommy had taken post on the front porch, watching as

his peers arrived. He didn't want to be out there greeting them, but he'd much rather be out front than in the house mingling with everyone, faking a good time. The night had only begun and already he wished nothing more than for it to end. His sour mood had turned into full-on depression. He had already been dreading the evening, but now that it was upon them, he felt worse than he had anticipated.

When Patrick Klein, the star quarterback he'd knocked out that one time showed up, things got even worse.

"Hey, Douche Canoe," Patrick said before taking a swig from the bottle of Bud Light he'd brought with him. He was flanked by the team's biggest linebacker and their starting running back—both boys were prime physical specimens and Tommy felt his balls shrivel up into his stomach. He'd been lucky the one time they'd fought, having gotten the drop on Patrick, but if he and his lackeys meant to cause trouble, there would be little he could do about it aside from hope they wouldn't cause any lasting, permanent brain damage.

Patrick must have taken notice of Tommy's body language because he laughed and said, "Relax, pussy, I'm not gonna hit you . . . right now."

The three football stars walked past Tommy, laughing up a storm as the running back shoulder-bumped Tommy, practically knocking him on his ass.

"Fucking dickheads," he muttered under his breath.

Patrick turned around and smiled. Tommy clenched his jaw. He hadn't intended to say it within earshot of the three stooges but now he had their attention for sure.

"See you around, Tommy," Patrick said with a wink before heading into the cabin.

Tommy exhaled a deep breath. Maybe he'd just leave.

He didn't want to be here anyway, and every minute he stayed he was risking the beating of a lifetime, especially once the jocks got liquored up. This was such a stupid idea.

But in the back of his mind, the part harboring the unseen guilt, he kind of wanted to stick around and take the beating. Didn't he deserve it? A good old-fashioned ass-whooping was still nothing compared to what he'd done to Joey. Nothing compared to jail time. Even if he ended up in the hospital, it was still not punishment enough for his sins.

The guilty part of him won out and he decided to stay. Let whatever happened tonight happen, he didn't give a fuck anymore.

Tommy sat down on one of the wooden deck chairs and unscrewed his flask. No beer for him tonight. And he wouldn't be drinking the piss in a plastic jug or the vodka being passed around. No sir, he'd gotten the good shit for himself, Knob Creek, and he intended on getting fucked-up beyond all belief.

A few hours had slipped away like a thief in the night and Patrick was feeling the effects of the alcohol. He'd passed good and buzzed, smashed through drunk, and was well on his way to being absolutely annihilated. The hangover from hell was on the horizon for sure. He walked along the lake with his two buddies, Zack and Ted. Truth be told, he hardly considered them buddies. The way they stuck to his heels like flies on shit was pathetic, but at the same time, it gave him power. Of course he didn't need the cronies to flex on his classmates, in a fair fight there weren't many who could take him on. He was tall, strong, and athletic. Not to mention, his father was something of a local boxing legend and had taught him how to throw hands at an early age.

The thought process brought to mind that little bitch, Tommy, and how he'd been the only person who'd ever had the audacity to sucker punch him. That was the lone blemish on his manhood, and it had only happened because he'd let his guard down. Still, his classmates had seen him get knocked out, and he figured he still owed Tommy one for that. He'd wanted to beat the brakes off him the very next day but a cooler head had prevailed. For no other reason than the fear of his own father, really. He wanted to get out of Budlong and he had a full ride to the University of Connecticut, but a suspension from school or a run-in with the police would for sure put the ice on that. And if he lost the scholarship, well, his old man, even in his late forties, was still capable of putting a real hurt on him. His old man was the only person he didn't think he could take one-on-one. Tommy had been lucky, but tonight, his luck would run out.

As time went on, Patrick hadn't quite forgotten about the embarrassment, but it was no longer at the forefront of his mind. There were other, more important things to focus on. Like sports and getting laid. The other teens at school knew better than to remind him about it, lest they be on the receiving end of his wrath. But when he'd passed Tommy on the porch and that fucking twerp had actually ran his mouth . . . Well, that had pissed him off. Patrick only planned to scare him. The look on the kid's face when he told him he'd see him later spoke volumes about who was really top dog. But now that he was all liquored up, Patrick thought maybe leaving the kid in fear wasn't enough. He could wallop Tommy and have zero consequences. The cops would never know. It's not like Tommy would run to the police and rat. Doing so would bring heat on the party; he would have to admit that he'd thrown it and provided alcohol to dozens of minors.

And there was also the matter of the little interrogation earlier in the year. Nothing had ever come of it, but everyone knew that Tommy had been questioned about Joey's death. It was something one of his teammates—who just happened to be the son of the police chief—had told him. Of course none of that amounted to guilt, but eventually whispers spread that Joey's death had been no accident, and the detectives wanted to pin something on Tommy but hadn't been able to.

So yeah, the kid would be a fool to try pressing charges if and when Patrick beat his ass, and the more his drunk mind went over it, he thought maybe the cops would be happy Tommy had gotten a taste of karma.

"Hey, wait right here," Zack said. "I'm gonna go take a piss in the woods real quick."

Patrick gave Zack a shove, harder than he meant to, knocking him off-balance. "Why? Afraid we're gonna see your little pecker? Just piss in the lake."

"Dude, that's gross," Ted chimed in.

Patrick sighed. "Shut the fuck up, Ted. Zack, stop being a pussy and piss in the lake. It's not like you've never done it. How many times have you just pissed in your shorts while you're swimming? Everyone does it."

"Yeah, but that's while I'm swimming. It's not the same. I don't want to just whip it out and piss."

"If you go in the woods to piss, I'm gonna tell everyone about what you slipped in Missy's drink at her party last week. You really want everyone to know you're a rapist?"

Zack's face went beet red. "I didn't rape her. I just gave her something to loosen her up a bit."

"She passed out and you took advantage of her. That's rape."

"I got them from you."

"You tell anyone that, they're not gonna believe you. And then I'm gonna kill you myself," Tommy said, taking one more swig of his beer before tossing the can onto the ground.

He was just busting balls when he told Zack he'd tell everyone about the stuff he had slipped in Missy's drink, but the moment Zack had brought up the source of the stuff, Patrick become deadly serious. He shoved his friend again. "Go take a fucking piss so we can go back to the party. I'm looking for a fight, so I can either beat your ass now, or we can all go beat the shit out of Tommy."

Zack must have seen the look in Patrick's eyes because he stopped complaining, walked over to the lake, whipped his dick out, and started pissing.

Patrick heard the steady stream hit the water, heard Zack moaning in near sexual ecstasy as he relieved his bladder. Zack stood over the water for a good amount of time. They'd pounded quite a few beers and the boy had only just broken the seal.

"Agghhhh! What the fuck?" Zack yelled.

"Man, shut the fuck up and hurry."

Zack yelled again, this time no words, just a bloodcurdling, primal scream.

Patrick and Ted rushed over to their friend, drunkenly stumbling to his side. At first, they didn't know what was going on. Zack's face was a rictus of pain and terror as he bent over, looking at his groin, swatting at the area while screaming.

Patrick looked down and echoed Zack's earlier outburst. "What the fuck?"

"Help," Zack managed to say. "Get this fucking thing off me.

A long, thick, black tendril ran from the lake to Zack's cock, where it appeared to enter his piss hole. His penis was swollen from the foreign invasion and looked like it was ready to burst at any second.

"Get that thing off him," Patrick yelled at Ted.

"Fuck that, I'm not touching his dick, or that thing. What the fuck, man. Why don't *you* do it."

Patrick certainly wasn't about to go near another man's dick, and he certainly wasn't going to touch . . . whatever the hell that thing was.

But neither of the boys had a chance to react.

Spiky protrusions burst through the skin of Zack's shaft, spraying scarlet. The head of his penis had erupted and now looked like a spent shotgun shell, flayed bits of flesh and sinew blown out and pouring blood.

The thing continued to pulse through Zack's mangled cock as it continued working its way through his urethra into the boy's body. He screamed, a guttural, inhuman noise, before mercifully passing out. His body fell backward, but the thing from the lake kept it suspended over the ground at an angle.

More protrusions burst from various points of his body. His anus, his legs, his stomach. Black ooze seeped from his eyes, his mouth, his nose, even his ears. It moved around his body, enveloping it, consuming the entirety until there was nothing left but a vaguely human-shaped black writhing mass. It all happened so quickly the other boys were frozen in shock.

"Run!" Ted shouted at last.

Patrick didn't take orders from anyone, but this situation was something else entirely and he didn't need to be told twice. Both boys turned around and took off running with their tails between their legs.

The ooze, finished with the consumption of Zack, broke apart and separated into two pieces. The smaller section retreated back into the lake, maneuvering through the water toward the other side, where one of the only summer families on the lake was holding a gathering and had even taken to partying with a few of the teens who had used a canoe to cross the lake.

The larger section glided effortlessly across the dirt in pursuit of the boys, following the trail they took that led through the woods back to the cabin.

Both boys, though in peak physical condition, were not making good time. The cabin was about a mile down the trail, which was nothing for either of them, but they had had too much to drink and were in no condition to make a run for their lives.

Patrick especially.

He was giving it his all to keep pace with Ted, who was naturally a stronger runner. Patrick was known for having a cannon arm, not for his ability to run down the field. Sneaking a quick glance behind him, he saw the black, tarry substance that had mangled and devoured his friend rapidly catching up, maneuvering over the rough trail just as easily as he assumed it glided through the water.

They needed a change of plan, maybe if they left the trail and cut through the woods they could create distance and make it back to the cabin. Just because it could handle the trail didn't mean it could make it through the copse of trees, shrubbery, and other natural obstacles.

At least he hoped that would be the case.

Through heaving breaths, he shouted, "Ted, go through the woods! Maybe we can lose it!"

The extra effort to bark orders almost caused him to yack, and he slipped a little farther behind Ted. For a moment, he thought his friend intended to keep to the path, but he suddenly cut right, through the line of trees and into the woods.

Patrick followed.

They continued the arduous task, the terrain slowing their speed considerably while also making it perilous. He hoped to God he wouldn't slip on a rock, take a branch to the face, or worse, fuck up his ankle by catching his foot on a root coming out of the ground. Any of those things could be the end of him.

Minutes that felt like hours crawled by and though their speed had slowed considerably, Patrick couldn't catch his breath. It took too much effort to navigate the obstacles in their way, and frankly, he was far too fucking drunk to keep going.

He looked back. The ooze was gone.

Had they lost it? Had it given up? Maybe. There was really no way to know, but his body had been pushed to the limit and his brain was telling him what he wanted to hear—that it had simply stopped pursuing them and slinked back into the lake, or wherever the hell it had come from.

"Ted, hold up. I think we're good," he said, hunched over with his hands on his thighs. It was a mistake, lowering his head like that. Anyone who knew anything about physical activity would tell you the best way to catch your breath and relax was to stand up straight with good posture, open up the lungs, and breathe slow, controlled breaths. But Patrick was drunk as hell and coming down from the full-on panic of an actual run for his life.

He vomited right there, chunks of food intermingled with the alcohol ejected from his stomach.

"Dude, shut the fuck up, you sound like you're fighting a bear," Ted said.

"Fuck . . . you."

He knew Ted was right; it wasn't the first time someone had made a comment about how loud he was when he threw up, but he couldn't help it. Of course he would puke silently if he could. The last thing he wanted was that thing hearing him. *Could* it hear him? He had no clue about the biological features of whatever the fuck that thing was, but it's not like he could magically stop his body from retaliating against the alcohol and sudden, rigorous physical activity.

A few minutes slipped by, and with them, the nausea.

"We gotta get back to the cabin," Patrick said, wiping his mouth with the back of his hand.

Ted pulled his phone from his pocket. "Yeah, we gotta call the cops, man. That was fucking crazy. What the fuck was that thing?"

"I don't know. I've never seen anything like it before." Images of Zack's mangled cock flashed through his mind. He recalled the way the black substance entered his friend's body before erupting out of it. The blood. There was so much blood.

"Fuck! I don't have any service out here," Ted said.

"What about at the cabin, did you have service there?"

"I don't know. I didn't check my phone then."

"Okay, we gotta go back there anyway. If it doesn't

work, *someone* has to have service. Or at least there might be Wi-Fi we can connect to."

"Yeah, you're right."

"Just give me another minute, man, I can hardly breathe right now."

Ted shook his head. "We don't have time, Pat. What if that thing comes back?"

"Did you see how fast it moved? If it was going to find us it already would have. I think we lost it."

Patrick could tell Ted wasn't buying it, but kept his objections to himself.

"All right, man, but hurry up. Please. We've gotta warn the others to stay out of the lake."

Ted was right and Patrick knew it. But he could only push himself so much. Especially after a night of heavy drinking. "Okay, but we gotta walk. I can't run anymore. Let's keep to the woods, we seem to have lost it that way."

"Bet," Ted said.

Behind them, leaves rustled. There was a rush of air as a black, spear-like projectile whizzed by Patrick's ear, narrowly missing when he turned to check out the noise.

"Jesus Christ, it's fucking back," Ted shouted.

Suddenly, Patrick kicked Ted on the side of his knee. There was a *snap* and his friend's leg buckled at an odd angle.

Ted screamed in pain, his face a rictus of anguish.

The old adage about not having to be faster than the bear, just faster than the next person ran through Patrick's head. "Sorry, man, but if it's me or you, it ain't gonna be me."

He took off running through the woods, toward the cabin with a renewed sense of self-preservation. If lady luck was on his side he would keep from getting sick until he was in the clear.

As he made his way through the woods, putting distance between him and the thing, he heard fading screams as the substance from the lake consumed his friend.

16

———

Jason Stanfield kept the throttle on the boat as his girlfriend, Calie, trailed behind him on water skis. Sitting behind him, his buddy, Jackson, and his girlfriend, Torie, were sipping their beers and passing a joint between them.

They were out in the middle of the lake, making sure to stay clear of the swimmers jumping off the docks. There were a lot of people partying at his family's portion of the lake tonight. They were throwing an end of summer get-together, and apparently there was a local party of high school graduates doing the same at one of the cabins on the other side of the lake. A few of the kids had taken some canoes over and joined the party, bringing with them plenty of beer and liquor.

Jason thought his father would have told them to kick rocks, but he had already tied one on and had been uncharacteristically welcoming of the teens.

Across the lake, Jason thought he'd heard screaming, but it was difficult to tell over the thumping of the music coming from his father's sound system and the little boat's engine. In the distance, he had seen what he thought to be more teenagers on the shore, but he couldn't be sure.

He turned the boat hard, not letting off the throttle until he had already cut the wheel. A stupid mistake. The alcohol had clouded his judgment and he heard Calie shriek, followed by a splash in the water.

He brought the boat to a halt, laughing. He knew she'd be fine. Calie was a strong swimmer and always wore a life jacket. She might be mad at him for being a bit careless but in the end, they'd be laughing it off.

Jackson and Torie laughed hysterically, pointing in the water where Calie had taken a spill. It was always funny when someone ate shit out on the lake.

Jackson made his way to the back of the boat, ready to help her up.

"Did you see that shit?" he asked. "She went head over heels, man. She's gonna whoop your ass when she gets up here."

Jason flashed a smile at his buddy. "Yeah, maybe. But she's gonna kick your ass, too, if you don't stop laughing."

"We can't help it, that was fucking hilarious," Torie said.

Jason saw Calie making her way to the boat, a big grin plastered across her face. That was good. It meant they could laugh it off instead of argue about his carelessness. They didn't argue often, and Calie had such a big heart that she often brushed things off quickly. Jason, by nature, was nonconfrontational and hated to be in any sort of argument, even if he knew it wouldn't last.

"Sorry, babe!" he shouted. "I took that turn a bit too hard."

"You think?" she snarked, now within an arm's reach.

Jason smiled at her and extended his hand, reaching over the side of the boat to help her in. She grasped it, but just as their fingers grazed each other, she quickly dropped below the surface. Jason's smile turned perplexed. She had a life vest on, how the hell could she drop below the surface like that?

She couldn't . . . unless . . .

Unless someone was in the water with her. But that couldn't be, could it? Jackson and Torie were here on the boat with him. Everyone partying at his house was too far away to realistically swim this far, and even if they could, they couldn't possibly make it here unseen, unheard. And who would do that, anyway?

Jason thought about the lake. There were no sharks in the lake, obviously. So what the hell could be going on?

Just as soon as she dipped below the surface, she popped back up, screaming bloody murder, "Help, Jason, help me!"

Her arms flailed, splashing water around her. "It hurts, something's got me, help!"

For an instant, he thought she was messing with him, but the look on her face told him otherwise. He jumped into the water and swam to Calie. As he arrived at her side he saw something dark slinking up her body. It was the color of onyx and seemed to cover most of her exposed skin. Her arms were completely black, and the substance worked its way up her neck, creeping closer to her mouth. He reached out for her, grabbing her hand and felt a blinding flash of pain as the thing morphed into a barbed appendage and speared through his palm.

"Fuck!" he screamed.

He grabbed at his hand instinctively, trying to pry the thing away, but it was no use. It crawled up his arm, which now felt as if it were on fire where the thing was attached to him. He could feel it eating away at his flesh, the pain unbearable. Sulfuric acid on the skin.

Torie and Jackson leaned over the edge of the boat. "What the hell is going on?" Jackson screamed.

Calie disappeared below the surface again but Jason didn't notice, he was off in his own world, searing pain making him oblivious to everything else around him. The thing had spread to his other arm and enveloped most of his body, leaving the entirety of him feeling like he was on fire despite being mostly submerged in the lake.

A protrusion shot off from the creature like a high caliber bullet, exploding Jason's head like a watermelon.

Jackson was peppered with the biological shrapnel. Blood, brain matter, and bits of bone splattered across his face.

Torie shrieked as the black ooze crawled up the side of the boat.

17

Jackie and Rowan were on the large outdoor patio. It was connected to the house and enclosed by walls, with large, screen windows making the area a great place to hang out when the weather was nice. It was connected to the living room, and at the moment, acted as an extension of the party. Jackie looked at her phone. It was late, almost one in the morning, but the party was still going strong. Many of the attendees had left, but there were quite a few present who showed no sign of leaving anytime soon. Jackie hoped that wasn't the case; she was ready to crash, but it was more than that. She'd hardly seen her brother all night and was worried about him. He'd been acting differently lately, even though they agreed to bury the hatchet and move on. She was hoping to have a heart-to-heart with him.

"You're thinking about Tommy again, huh?" Rowan asked.

"That obvious?"

"Yeah. Listen, he's gonna be fine, I really believe that.

But I know he's your brother and you're gonna worry. That's normal. But I think he just needs time. Everything is still fresh."

Jackie frowned. Rowan didn't know Tommy the way she did. They'd all been through the same traumatic night together but at the end of the day, it was Tommy, not them, who had to live with the fact that he'd thrown the punch that landed Joey in the water. On the surface, he might seem like he was holding up, but she knew better. No matter how often you tell yourself and others you're fine, holding yourself responsible for your friend's death couldn't be good for you.

"I appreciate it, I really do, but he's not fine. I know him. He's acting differently and I'm starting to worry he's gonna do something drastic."

Rowan nodded her head. "What, like you think he's gonna hurt himself?"

"I don't know. Maybe. Maybe not. But I'm worried that I'm gonna lose him. I think he wants to cut ties with Budlong and be rid of all this."

Rowan gripped Jackie's shoulders, pressed her forehead to hers. "Babe, he's always going to be your brother. You guys will always be close. If he needs space, let him have space."

Jackie smiled at Rowan and leaned in, kissing her girlfriend passionately.

"Am I interrupting something?" Tommy asked, entering the patio from the outside door.

Jackie pushed away and smoothed her shirt. "Hey, I was just wondering what happened to you. I haven't seen you all night."

"Yeah, you look like you were really worried."

"Tommy, don't be a jerk. It's not what it looks like. We weren't out here making out. She's been worried about you all night," Rowan said.

"I'm sorry. I've been out walking around the woods, clearing my head. This was a mistake. It doesn't feel right. I don't know why Mr. Harrison wanted us to do this. Something about it just doesn't make sense."

"Is that all?" Jackie asked.

"Not really. I ran into Patrick and his dipshit friends earlier. Kinda figured If I ran into them they'd get it over with and put me out of my misery. But then I thought about it and decided I wasn't really feeling up to getting jumped by three football players, so I kinda hid out for a bit."

"Why didn't you say something?" Rowan asked.

"Say what? To who? You two gonna fight them with me? I don't need your protection. It's just, everyone's drinking, and they were already tipsy when they got here. And . . . I kinda pissed them off earlier. Didn't want to give them a reason, that's all."

There was a commotion coming from the woods behind the house. The three of them turned and saw Patrick stumbling toward them. She sensed Tommy tense up next to her, reached out to put a hand on his shoulder. A small gesture she hoped would set his mind at ease, though she knew better.

He burst onto the patio and Jackie knew something wasn't right. He didn't look pissed. He didn't look like he was coming to ruin Tommy's day.

He looked petrified.

"Listen, man, I don't want any trouble," Tommy said.

Patrick shook his head, tried to speak, but he was

clearly out of breath and having trouble getting the words to leave his mouth. He was covered in puke and . . . blood?

"Patrick, take a deep breath. What's wrong?" Rowan asked.

He looked at her, tried to compose himself. It took a bit before he responded, but when he did, Jackie couldn't believe the words that came out of his mouth.

He explained everything that happened—how something had gotten Ted and Zack, leaving out how he had sacrificed his friend to save his own bacon, only pausing to dry heave and wipe specks of spittle from his mouth.

"How much did you have to drink, man?" Tommy asked.

"What, you don't believe me? I'm not making this up and if you call me a liar again you're gonna be shitting out your teeth for a week. We've got unfinished business."

Tommy stepped to Patrick, clearly pissed, but Jackie stepped between them. She wasn't about to watch her brother fight this kid. She remembered what happened the last time she couldn't stop Tommy from fighting someone and wasn't about to witness another horrible accident.

"Nobody is calling you a liar. I think Tommy was just saying that you've had a lot to drink and maybe something happened, but not exactly what you think you saw." Jackie said.

Patrick sucked his teeth. "I know what I saw. They're dead. We gotta call the cops, get someone out here. That fucking thing is in the woods. It came out of the lake and if *someone* doesn't do *something* then more people are going to die.

There was a spattering noise off to the side. Jackie looked behind Patrick and saw a massive, dark blob plastered against the windows. It seeped through the openings in the screens and reformed as a solid mass on their side of the windows, while a much larger portion of it spread along the outside of the cabin, blocking off the exit from that side of the building.

She screamed and the other three turned to look.

"I fucking told you! Run!" Patrick shouted before shouldering his way through the three of them, disappearing into the house.

"What the hell is that?" Tommy asked.

"Jesus. That must be whatever got Zack and Ted. Go! We've gotta get everyone out of here!"

With the thing hot on their heels, they turned and ran into the cabin.

18

———

Tommy was the first through the door, Rowan and Jackie trailing behind him. He heard one of them slam the door shut, but judging by the way the thing had oozed through the screen windows, he didn't expect that would do much to keep the thing at bay.

He heard angry shouts in front of him as Patrick shoved his way through the crowd, making his hasty retreat.

Tommy stopped in the center of the main living room, where most of the partygoers were still congregated. It was late but the place was still jam-packed. He shouted over the music, "Everyone, listen up! The party is over. There's been an accident. The police are on their way."

The few people standing nearby gave him an odd look but made no effort to listen.

"Man, stop being a fucking buzzkill," said a tall, blond boy next to him.

Shit. This wasn't going to work. The music was too loud, too many people lost in conversation.

The music.

He ran to the sound system and pulled the plug from the wall. There were groans and angry shouts from the crowd.

"The party is over. The cops are on their way!" he repeated, telling the same lie. It wasn't exactly true, but as soon as he got everyone out of there and they were on the road, he would dial 911. He had no intention of waiting around to place the call from the cabin's Wi-Fi.

"Turn the fucking tunes back on! Who made you the fucking party captain?" Another angry shout from the crowd.

Suddenly, screams came from the front of the cabin.

Tommy shoved his way through the crowd and witnessed what had caused the commotion.

Patrick was in front of the now open front door, hovering, his feet dangling a few feet off the ground.

Except he wasn't hovering, he was held in the air by some sort of black, spear-like object that had impaled him in the chest and punched all the way through his shoulder blades. Blood gushed from the wounds, puddling on the floor beneath him.

The room was in utter chaos. All the remaining partiers fled in every direction, attempting to flee the thing that had killed Patrick.

The thing swatted its spear-arm to the side, tossing Patrick like a rag doll. His body crashed into the wall, cratering the cheap faux wood, leaving his discarded corpse crumpled on the floor.

As the kids all scattered to the wind, the thing shifted and morphed, shooting black ooze projectiles, picking them off like fish in a barrel.

One of the fleeing teens opened the window to escape, his path blocked by the substance that had surrounded the house. He screamed and the ooze shot a blob of itself at his face, drowning his pleas for help as it devoured his flesh, traveling along his body, leaving nothing but blood and tattered scraps of clothing in its wake.

The larger humanoid shape that had murdered Patrick grew even more massive, now a behemoth seven feet tall with arms and legs the size of logs. It stomped through the main room, clobbering and smashing the fleeing students. There was nowhere to run, they were all as good as dead.

One of them knocked a lantern off the mantel. It crashed to the ground and the carpet caught fire.

The flames caught quickly, spreading throughout the room. The creature backed away from the fire, screeching.

Someone grabbed Tommy's shoulder and he spun around. It was Jackie, tears streaming down her face.

"We've gotta get out of here, now!" The words came out a garbled mess between sobs.

Tommy looked around, saw his sister was right. But where to? The cabin was surrounded by whatever the hell that thing was, and to make matters worse, despite seemingly being afraid of the fire, the behemoth was still laying waste to everyone around it.

"Where's Rowan?" he asked.

Jackie looked to her right at a body on the floor.

"Jesus Christ. Not Rowan."

"She's gone. And we will be, too, if we don't move, now."

Tommy tried to think, but between the screams of dying teens, the now roaring inferno, and the screeches from that thing, his mind was muddied.

"The basement! Maybe we can get out through the bulkhead." He had no idea if they could get out through the bulkhead. The thing had enveloped the cabin somehow, stretching and expanding until it had covered the entirety of it, but maybe it hadn't covered the bulkhead? The idea seemed paper-thin and he knew it, but what other choice did they have?

"Okay," she said. "Let's try it. We don't have any other options.

Jackie grabbed his hand and they made for the door, but an idea popped into Tommy's head. "Wait," he said, letting go of her hand. He ran to the fireplace and grabbed the heat mitt and poker before stripping his shirt off and wrapping it around the end of the iron tool. He shoved the shirt into the nearest flame, lighting it.

"Maybe we can use this," he said.

They made their way to the basement, Jackie tailing behind Tommy, who led the way with the flaming poker.

19

———

The basement was dark but the flaming poker lent an eerie illumination, the flickering flames licking away at the darkness. Tommy slammed the door behind him not a moment too soon. A sharp projectile pierced the door, slicing his shoulder open. "Shit," he cried out.

Ooze from the projectile stuck to his flesh, creeping along it. He could feel it burning as it ate away at his skin. "Jackie, help me!"

"Give me the poker," she said.

Tommy did as he was told.

"This is gonna hurt," she said.

"It already hurts, just fucking do it!"

Jackie pressed the flaming cloth against the black substance. The creature outside the door shrieked in pain. Tommy heard his flesh sizzle as the thing, along with his flesh, burned.

Jackie pulled the flame away. Beads of sweat dripped down Tommy's forehead. That hurt. A lot. He hoped she hadn't burned him too badly, but if they didn't get the hell out of there soon, a burn would be the least of his troubles.

"Where's the bulkhead?" she asked. "Did you come down here earlier?"

"It's to the left. Follow me." He grabbed the makeshift torch from his sister and once again led the way.

He heard the door shatter, splinters of wood peppering them from behind. "Keep going, don't stop," he told his sister.

They moved through the basement as fast as they could, stumbling over various stored items.

"There!" Jackie said.

They ran to the bulkhead and Tommy stopped, deflated. The sliding bar was held in place with a combination lock. Their luck had run out.

The siblings spun around. "There's gotta be something we can use to bust it open," Jackie said. They stuck together. It would have been quicker to split up, but with only one torch it would do them little good to separate.

Tommy's shoulder was numb and he wasn't sure if that was good or bad. What if that thing had given him some sort of infection, or had poisoned him? What the hell was it, anyway?

"Over here," he said. "Looks like a tool rack." They sifted through the shelves of the metal rack, looking for anything that could work.

Jackie picked up a hammer. "What about this?" she asked.

"Found something even better." Tommy held up bolt cutters, the long red arms bright against the flickering light of the fire, which was beginning to fade.

"Jackie, give me your shirt, this is starting to go out."

"I'm not walking around in a bra!" she said.

"If you don't give me the damn shirt neither of us will be walking out of here."

"Fine," she said, pulling her shirt over her head.

"*Tommmmmyyyyy*," something croaked.

"What the hell was that?" Jackie asked.

"I don't fucking believe it."

Tommy backed away, holding out the torch. Through the dimly lit basement, the creature was stalking toward them. But it wasn't a lumbering hulk like it had been upstairs, it was smaller and more defined. The thing walking forward looked an awful lot like Joey, but the features weren't right. They were there, not quite right, but unmistakably Joey.

"Joey . . ." Jackie said.

"That's not Joey. We've gotta go. Now!"

They ran back to the bulkhead. "Here, give me the bolt cutters," Jackie said.

Tommy traded them for a can of WD-40 she had snagged off the shelf.

Jackie opened the cutters and clamped them down on the lock, wrenching and squeezing the tool, but it was no use.

The thing was closer now, its form shifting continuously, taking the face of the people it had killed. Many of them Tommy knew from school, but there were quite a few he'd never seen before. He waved the torch in front of him, hoping to scare the creature. Fire had hurt it earlier, but if it felt fear, it wasn't showing it.

The thing settled on Joey's shape again. "*You killllllled-dddd me*," it said. The thing's voice was awful, like nothing he'd ever heard. It was obviously some sort of shape-shifter, and could even replicate voices, though with an inhuman quality.

"Get back. Don't come any closer." Tommy felt as stupid as the command sounded. He always cursed at movies when the characters said that, as if the thing threatening their lives would listen. It seemed so fake, so forced, and here he was, reduced to the same stupidity. The creature was now backlit by flames that had travelled from the main floor to the basement, devouring everything in the fire's path.

"Tommy, I can't get it."

"Let me try."

They swapped positions and implements. Jackie stood close to Tommy. He didn't blame her, he didn't want to be near that thing either.

Its arm—now a long black club—extended and swatted the torch out of Jackie's grasp, the poker skittering across the floor.

"Got it!" Tommy said. A loud *snap* and the lock fell to the ground. He pulled the sliding lock to the side and forced the bulkhead open.

"It's clear!" Tommy said. "It's not blocking the door. You go first."

Tommy let his sister sidle past him and she immediately screamed as the ooze that was enveloping the house quickly approached from both sides of the bulkhead.

Tommy acted quickly, grabbing the torch and the W-40 off the ground and running up to Jackie, spraying the can at the torch. There was a loud *whoosh* as the liquid caught fire, spitting flames at the encroaching ooze.

The creature in the basement shrieked in pain as the

ooze outside the house retreated, not much, but enough for Jackie to escape.

Tommy felt a dagger of pain along the back of his foot and fell face-first. A black projectile pierced his ankle and protruded all the way through the other side. His chin smacked the steps, clacking his teeth together. He spit out a loose tooth and blood gushed from his mouth.

Jackie turned around. "Tommy," she yelled as she ran back and reached for him.

The black projectile in his foot was already traveling up his leg, devouring his flesh as the thing stalked forward, its arm now the shape of a large scythe.

Death was upon him, there was no hope. He saw the flames and noticed they were dangerously close to propane tanks lying on the floor next to the tool shelves. This was it. He was as good as dead, and Jackie would be too if he didn't stop her.

"Jackie. Forget about me, the place is gonna blow!" He pointed at the tanks.

"What?" she yelled.

"Go, now! It's gonna blow!"

She must have seen where he was pointing because her eyes practically bulged from her head. The ooze outside the house was slowly creeping back, damaged from the flames but ready for round two.

Tommy handed her the torch and the WD-40. "I love you," he said. "I'm sorry for everything. Now get the fuck out of here."

Tears rolled down Jackie's cheeks. "I love you, too," she said, and then she was gone.

Tommy could hear her spraying the WD-40, using it as a flame thrower to clear a path.

Tommy pissed himself as the thing raised its appendage in the air.

"I love you too, Joey," he said and closed his eyes as the scythe-arm descended.

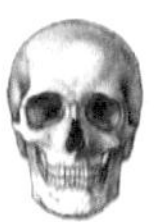

Jackie sprayed the can liberally to and fro, hoping it wouldn't explode in her hand. The ooze retreated. She pressed the nozzle again but nothing happened. The flame was dying out on the torch. She had to make it to the car quickly or the thing would be on her again, and this time she would have no defense.

In the parking lot now, she could see the car and then she felt an immense wave of heat on her back and heard a loud *whoomp*.

Her ears rang and everything went black.

20

When Jackie's eyes opened there was nothing but a blinding white light. *Heaven*, she thought, exactly as she'd heard it described. She wasn't a believer, but maybe God didn't care about that, only that you were a good person. It made sense. Over the ages, religion had been twisted and reshaped as a methodology to control human behavior.

But she soon began to feel a dull pain and the brightness faded as her eyes adjusted. She could hear mechanical whirring noises and beeps.

"She's awake!" a man exclaimed from somewhere off to the side.

She turned to the voice. Her father and mother were bedside.

"Oh, baby, we were so worried," her mother said.

Jackie tried to lift her arm, but found the task too difficult. It was wrapped in bandages and now that she was alert, the sense of pain was growing.

"Honey, try not to move too much. You're in the hospital. You've been badly burned. They had to airlift you to Rhode Island Hospital to treat you. They told us you'd make a full recovery, but it's going to be a long and painful road. At first . . . they weren't sure—" Her mother began to sob, couldn't finish her sentence. Dad took her in his arms.

"Where's Tommy?" Jackie asked.

Neither of her parents replied. Dad continued to hold Mom as she wept in his arms.

Jackie's heart raced. No, it couldn't be true. *Tommy had to be okay*, she told herself. But in her heart, she knew Tommy was gone. She'd tried to help him but he refused, knowing that if she tried they would both perish.

"There was an explosion, baby. Something caught fire and spread throughout the cabin. When it hit the propane tanks . . ." Dad shook his head. "They're still investigating the cause of the fire but it was bad. So many kids . . . they didn't make it."

They shed their tears as a family. Mom and Dad mourning the loss of their son, while Jackie cried for not only her brother, but Rowan, Joey, and the rest of her friends.

A knock on the door interrupted their grieving and a man wearing a black suit entered the room.

"Get out," her father said.

"Mr. Ross, it is imperative that I speak with your daughter. We need to get to the bottom of this. She is the only eyewitness. We're hoping she could shed light on the specifics of a very questionable tragedy. One that has claimed the lives of everyone present, aside from your daughter," the visitor explained.

"She won't be talking to anyone right now. You're

going to have to wait. Our son is dead, show some respect," her father said, getting in the man's face.

"There is no need for hostility, Mr. Ross. I'll give you time, but I only have so much patience. The sooner she can answer my questions the sooner I can get to the bottom of this. More lives could be in danger," the man said, closing the door behind him with a nod.

"Who was that?" Jackie asked.

"Agent Roberts," her father answered. "I don't know what he could possibly want with you. The police and fire marshal are conducting an investigation of the explosion. He wouldn't even tell me what agency he was with. Do you know why he would want to speak with you, baby?"

Jackie shook her head. "No clue."

The words "More lives could be in danger" sent a chill up her spine.

Jackie knew exactly why the man wanted to speak with her.

She wished she had died alongside her brother.

COMING SOON

JOHN LYNCH
THE
DINER

AFTERWORD

I'm glad to be done with this book. Not because I don't like it, I really enjoyed writing it, and I hope that you enjoyed reading it. But this one took a long time, for various reasons. This was to be the followup to my debut novel, The Warrior Retreat.

Instead, this ended up being my seventh book. So what happened? Well, all the other projects happened. I was about 10k words into this book when Jay Bower, John Durgin, and myself decided to work together for The Conservator's Collection, which featured my novella, Expiration of Sentence. With that out of the way, I decided to challenge myself to write an idea I had before I'd even written The Warrior Retreat, so Peril Beneath the Surface was set aside again and I began work on Christmas Eve Carnage.

After finished the first Carnage book, I had intended on finishing this, but I found that I'd lost the plot, and the characters after setting it aside. So I rewrote the book from scratch, writing about half of it, before I started writing

Christmas Eve Carnage 2, leaving Peril waiting in the depths once more.

With Carnage 2 halfway finished, Jay Bower and I decided to work together once more, and that project became Sleeper Train. I wanted to get back to Peril, but there was a problem, I HAD to finish Carnage 2 so I could get it out for the holiday season.

So again, Peril was pushed aside while I toiled away at finishing Carnage 2, which took far longer than it should have due to personal life problems I had been going through.

And when I finished that, finally, it was time to get back to peril. But there was another problem, I had the manuscript, but my notes were gone, and when I tried finishing the book, I felt I had lost the vibe. So, once again, I started from scratch and wrote the book over.

This would be the last rewrite, however. I buckled down and made it my priority to finish the book and not set it aside for anything else. But of course, that wasn't the case. I went on a writer's retreat earlier in the year and began work on a new project which you should see by the end of the year. That would be the last sidestep, as I returned hoe from the retreat and finished the book.

I hope you enjoy it, and thank you for reading my books. It means the world to me.

5-1-2025

JWL

ABOUT THE AUTHOR

John Lynch is a horror writer from Rhode Island. His works have been nominated for awards such as the Imad-jinn award, and the Splatterpunk award. When he's not writing he's usually buried in a book or at the gym, torturing himself.

For signed books and merch visit
    Johnlynchbooks.bigcartel.com

ACKNOWLEDGMENTS

Thank you to my good friends, Aron Beauregard, Daniel Volpe, John Durgin, and Jay Bower. Writing is a lonely task, but having a few authors in my close circle makes it less lonely.

Thank you to Christian Bentulan for the amazing cover, and Danielle Yeager of Hack and Slash editing for cleaning up my mess. The both of you put the final touches on this book that make it sing.

Thank you to Kiera, who has been here from the ground up. Without your early support of The Warrior Retreat, the rest of the books may never have followed.

A special thank you to Rachael, who brightens things up.

To everyone reading this book, whether this is your first book of mine, or you have been reading them all, thank you. You make it possible for me to continue doing what I love.

PATREON SUPPORTERS

Thank you to the following Patreon supporters!

Andy
Charlotte
Gage
Kayla
Mary
Molly
Sara
Nik

ALSO BY JOHN LYNCH

The Warrior Retreat

Expiration of Sentence

Woe To Those Who Dwell on Earth

Christmas Eve Carnage

Sleeper Train